ROPING YOUR HEART

Formatting and Interior Design by Bella Media Management.

First Pink Zebra Publishing Paperback Edition

13 Digit ISBN: 978-1480298538

ROPING YOUR HEART

CHEYENNE MCCRAY

PINK ZEBRA PUBLISHING
SCOTTSDALE, ARIZONA

PROLOGUE

Cat Hayden sat up in bed, waiting for Dr. Ross to come in. A dagger of pain plunged through her head, she felt as if the slash across her face was burning, and like every bone in her skull had been smashed. Her chest hurt and her bandaged ribs ached as she breathed.

She refused to look in the mirror. She didn't want to see the bandages around her face and head and acknowledge the damage that they covered, nor her bare scalp where her black hair had been partially shaved away.

The backs of her eyes ached, adding to the pain in her head. She had to force herself not to scratch the incision where she'd had brain surgery. Even though there are no nerve endings inside the skull, it itched like crazy.

The doorknob to the room turned and she tried to scoot up

farther in the bed but the pain in her body was too great.

Dr. Ross closed the door behind him. He was carrying a large envelope and a clipboard. "How are you doing today?"

Cat shrugged. "All right." Her speech slurred, sending a rush of frustration through her. She tried to swallow, but her throat hurt from the tube that had been there.

"We have the results back." He took CAT scans from the large envelope he'd been carrying and clipped them to an x-ray viewer that he turned on. She had to move her head as she watched him because her peripheral vision was off.

Images of her skull and brain were on the scans and he pointed to a couple of spots on one of the images on the film as he spoke. "As we knew, your skull is fractured." He continued and gave her technical terms she didn't understand before he ended with, "There's some irreparable damage, Cat."

Her skin prickled and the pressure in her head increased. "What does that mean?"

"What it comes down to is this." He set the clipboard and the large envelope aside and sat on the rolling swivel stool and met her eyes. "You shouldn't ride horses anymore or do anything where there's a danger that you could fall and hit your head. Next time, you might not be so lucky."

She couldn't hold back a tear and she wiped it away with her fingertips. "No more riding?"

"Especially not the kinds of riding you do," he said firmly. "Barrel racing and any other rodeo activities are out. As a matter of fact, you need to stay away from any rides that a pregnant woman must avoid. It's too jarring for the healing brain."

Heat washed over Cat's skin and she felt another tear trying to escape. Rodeo was a huge part of her life and had been ever since she could first ride a horse.

"What about just…riding?" Her hand trembled so hard that she had a hard time pushing hair behind her ear. She hated the uncontrollable shaking that made it difficult to do anything that required fine motor skills. "I could ride a gentle mount where there's little danger of being thrown."

"The horse could get spooked by a rattlesnake or any other number of things." The doctor's gaze was steady as he studied her. "It's not worth taking the chance."

She bit down on her lower lip. "What would you tell someone who was injured in a car accident? Not to drive anymore nor to even ride in a car because there's the danger of being in another accident?"

Dr. Ross stood. "When it comes down to it, it's up to you, Cat. But stay away from rodeo. You don't want to end up with serious brain damage."

"What else?" She needed to get away from the subject of riding.

"You may have vision issues for some time." He picked up her chart and glanced at it before looking at her again. "As far as your headaches are concerned, because of the location of the injury, they should subside as you heal. However, you could have migraines for the rest of your life. Only time will tell."

She couldn't bring herself to say anything as he told her she would be starting both occupational and physical therapy, as well as speech and vision therapy. He would be back to check on her tomorrow. She just nodded and held back more tears as she sat propped up in bed.

Yesterday, the plastic surgeon had told her they would do their best to repair the damage to her face, but the gouge across her face was so deep they probably wouldn't be able to fix it. Because of the way her face was damaged, by the time they finished reconstructive surgery she might look entirely different.

When she had control of her emotions and the doctor had left the room, she turned her head to the side and stared at the wall for a long time.

CHAPTER 1

"Great job, Demi." Cat shifted in her saddle and smiled at the girl astride a Quarter horse as she trotted away from the barrels. Cat glanced at the stopwatch she held. "That's your fastest time yet."

Demi grinned and the other 4-H kids in the horse club cheered and clapped. "The trick you showed me really helped, Ms. Hayden. Thanks."

For a moment Cat thought about Melanie and she felt the familiar ache in her heart. Her daughter would have been Demi's age and maybe she would have competed in rodeo, too.

"You're going to win the next competition for sure," Amy, Demi's best friend, was saying as Cat brought her attention back to the 4-H'ers.

Demi dismounted. "I need to get more practice in before the Flagstaff Junior Rodeo."

Today was Cat's first day as leader of the horse club and she was just getting to know the kids. She'd recently moved back to Prescott and an old friend had asked her to take over as leader of the small group.

"You're an excellent rider." Cat dismounted from Dolly, the horse she'd been riding, as she spoke to Demi. "Where do you practice?"

"On our ranch." Demi pushed up the brim of her straw western hat. She was a petite girl of fourteen with blonde hair pulled back into a braid. "My dad set up a practice ring when I was just a kid."

The six teens in the horse club were sitting on the wood rail of the practice ring or leaning up against it. The kids ranged in age from thirteen to sixteen.

A couple of the 4-H'ers lived close enough to ride their own horses to Folsom Ranch. Those who lived farther away used three of the Folsoms' horses that were well trained for all of the rodeo events. Gretchen and Dolly were trained for women's and girl's competitions. Shelton worked better with the men's and boy's events.

When they'd settled down, Cat looped Dolly's reins over a wood rail and smiled at the group as she moved in front of them. "I know you all have been around horses for a long time and you feel confident you know what to do. But, safety should always be your first priority." She looked from one kid to the next. "I'm going to share with you how I got this scar."

The kids focused on Cat.

"When I was nineteen, I worked in southern Arizona with a

rancher, rehabilitating horses, and got into a tangle with a gelding named Firestorm." Cat touched the scar on her face. "The horse won."

Now, she definitely had the kids' attention.

"I made the mistake of trying to work with the horse alone when I knew better." Cat stuck her hands in her back pockets. "Firestorm decided he wanted to kill me. He knocked me down and started rearing up and stomping on me."

One of the members was wide-eyed. "What happened?"

"In addition to this scar, I ended up with multiple fractures, broken ribs, a cracked skull, and part of my face crushed." Cat rocked back on her boot heels. "Probably the worst of all, is that I sustained a brain injury and had to have brain surgery. That was eighteen years ago, and I'm pretty much recovered from all of that."

"It must have been so painful." Amy's eyes were big. "Did you have to have plastic surgery as well?"

Cat nodded. "I had a lot of surgeries and had to go through three years of physical therapy and vision therapy."

"Were you afraid of horses after that?" Demi asked.

Cat paused for a moment. "The first time back on a horse was the hardest. I kept seeing flashes of what had happened and reliving it in my mind. But, you could never keep me off a horse forever."

A few of the kids nodded in agreement.

Cat continued, "The doctor didn't want me to ride at all because of the type of brain injury, he said that another accident could possibly kill me." She gave a little smile. "But, like I said, you can't keep me off a horse."

"That's awful," Amy said.

Demi let out her breath. "I can't imagine not being able to do something I love. I would be just like you—no one could keep me off a horse."

Cat nodded. "Because of the damage done and the three years of physical therapy, I had to quit competition." She pushed her hand through her hair. "I was a champion barrel racer and rodeo was a big part of my life. It was devastating to lose that."

Brett, a sixteen-year-old boy, asked, "Were you ever afraid to work with horses again?"

She shook her head. "I'm very careful now and I don't rehabilitate horses. I'm not telling you not to go down that path," she continued. "But I would caution you when it comes to being in a similar situation. I probably wouldn't have suffered the extent of injuries that I did if I had waited for the other handler to work with Firestorm and me. By the time the handler and a ranch hand got the horse off me, it was almost too late."

Neal tilted his head to the side. "So, always have someone with you when you're training horses?"

"It's a good idea," Cat said. "An untrained or formerly abused horse can be dangerous."

The kids nodded.

"My mom's here." Amy got down from the wood rail she'd been sitting on as a truck drove up. "I've got to go."

Cat glanced at her watch. "Looks like we're finished for the day," she said to the other kids as another car came down the dirt road to Folsom Ranch where the 4-H'ers met for the horse club.

"I'll brush down Gretchen and Dolly and put them up." Demi turned as she held both horses' reins and the trio headed toward barn.

"I'll take care of Shelton and help Demi," Brett said, and when Cat nodded, he took the reins of the gelding. In a few long strides he caught up with Demi.

The rest of the kids said goodbye as their rides came and Cat waved to them as they drove away.

A red truck approached, kicking up dust as the last kid left, with the exception of Demi and Brett who were still in the barn. Since Brett's vehicle was here, this was probably Demi's ride. Smiling and humming to herself, Cat walked toward the truck. She planned to talk to Demi's parents about her talent.

The truck rolled to a stop and the driver parked before climbing out. A tall figure strode around the vehicle from the driver's side and Cat came to a stop. Her heart pounded and her throat grew dry.

Blake McBride.

A Stetson shadowed his eyes and he had matured over the last nineteen years, but she knew it was him with everything she had. Her body tingled as she studied him and her heart rate picked up. His shoulders were broader and he was more filled out. Even though he wore a work shirt and snug Wrangler jeans, she knew his muscles were well defined and sculpted beneath the clothing. His shirtsleeves were rolled up, showing the tanned skin of his forearms and his collar was open at his throat. His jaws were stubbled, giving him a rougher look.

She felt a flush of heat throughout her at seeing him again. The years had flown by but it was as if no time had passed at all. Just looking at him, she felt like a teenager again.

Blake hesitated before he headed straight toward her, a smile softening his hard features and putting a light in his green eyes.

He came to a stop in front of her and held out his hand. "I'm Blake McBride."

"Hi, Blake." She straightened as she tilted her head to look up at the big man and she took his hand. "I don't think you recognize me."

The warmth of his hand traveled through her body as he studied her. "Your voice…your mannerisms…and your eyes. You have the same beautiful golden eyes and black hair of someone I cared a lot for." It was like a light dawned on him. "Cat?"

Surprise flowed through her. "It's me."

He looked stunned as he slowly released her hand. "I know it's been a long time, but no, I didn't recognize you. Not by your looks."

She kept her hands at her side even though she automatically wanted to touch the thick scar across her face. To hide it.

"Damn, it's good to see you." He caught her off guard by bringing her into his embrace and hugging her. He smelled wonderful, of sun-warmed flesh and leather. She felt an instant of comfort and belonging before she pushed the feelings away and stepped back. "Hell, it's been nineteen years," he said.

"It's good to see you, too." She took a deep breath as she sought to change the subject away from her looks. "So, what brings you to the Folsom Ranch?"

"My daughter." He looked toward the barn. "I'm not surprised she's still in the barn. The longer she can be around horses, the happier she is."

Cat's eyes widened slightly and her lips parted. "Demi is your daughter?"

The look of pride in his eyes was unmistakable. "Yep."

An ache came out of nowhere, squeezing her heart. "So, you're married?"

"Divorced." His features hardened almost imperceptibly and anger sparked in his eyes. He tried to hide it, but it was there. Apparently his divorce had not been pleasant.

The anger caught her off guard. "I'm sorry."

He studied her features and her face burned as she thought about what he might be thinking. From the time she was young up until the ordeal with the horse, she'd always been told she was beautiful. What had happened then had changed that.

He reached up and brushed his fingers over her scarred cheek as he echoed her thoughts. "What happened?"

A shiver ran through her at his touch. For a moment it was as if no time had passed and it was just the two of them alone in the world…she was eighteen and her heart had belonged to him. He had been her refuge. He'd been everything to her. And then she'd ruined it all.

She fought to bring herself back to the present and away from old memories. She shrugged, then told him the brief story she'd just told the kids. She didn't mention that the brain trauma still caused debilitating migraines. After eighteen years, she'd recovered from everything else.

"I'm sorry, honey." As if compelled, he trailed his fingers from the scar on her cheek to her ear and gently stroked her hair behind it. "That must have been hell."

Even though it had been so long since they'd been together, the tension between them was strong. His gaze lingered on her mouth as if he wanted to kiss her.

He stepped back and shook his head. "It's like no time has

passed at all."

She tilted her head to the side. "Even though I don't look the same?"

He gave a slow nod. "It doesn't matter a damned bit that you look a little different."

"A little different?" She shook her head even as his words echoed in her mind. "You didn't even recognize me."

"You know that a part of me did." He studied her eyes. "You're just as beautiful as you ever were. You're still KitCat to me."

A rush of heat went through her. Even though he'd never lied or exaggerated as long as she'd known him, that statement wasn't true.

"Dad?" Demi's voice came from behind Blake and he turned to face his daughter. "You know Ms. Hayden?"

He settled his arm around Demi's shoulders. "A long time ago, Cat was my girlfriend." It surprised Cat that he hadn't evaded the question or told the girl simply that they were old friends.

Demi looked from one of them to the other. "How long ago?"

"We were both eighteen," Cat said.

"Before Daddy met my mother," Demi said before her lips tightened. There was something in her eyes that was hard to read, as if the subject of her mother was something she didn't want to talk about and she was sorry she had even brought it up.

"Your daughter is a talented barrel racer." Cat glanced between the two of them. "I'm impressed."

"Thank you, Ms. Hayden." The girl's features brightened. "I've loved barrel racing since I was old enough for my dad to let me do it. I always liked watching the girls in the junior rodeos."

Blake looked at his daughter with pride gleaming in his eyes.

Cat assumed that the girl must look like her mother because she didn't favor Blake or his brothers. The McBrides tended to be dark-haired whereas Demi was blonde with freckles across her nose and she had eyes the same brown as redwood, almost cinnamon in color.

Cat thought again about Melanie with her dark hair and ready smile.

Demi looked at her father. "I've got homework, Dad."

He nodded. "Then we'd better get you home."

"Goodbye, Ms. Hayden," Demi said with a smile before she turned and walked to the truck that Blake had been driving.

Blake met Cat's gaze again. "It's good to see you."

Cat offered him a smile. "I imagine I'll see you at the next horse club meeting."

"I'm sure you will." He touched the brim of his hat, then turned and headed back to the truck where Demi was waiting.

The pounding of her heart hadn't slowed down from the first moment she'd seen him. Not until his truck was traveling down the road, kicking up dust in its wake, did her heart rate start going back to normal. She was barely aware of sixteen-year-old Brett walking up to stand beside her. He must have just finished putting up Shelton. His truck was still parked beside her own.

She and Brett watched Blake and Demi driving away from the Folsom Ranch, until they couldn't see the truck anymore.

CHAPTER 2

Monday morning, Cat rested her head on her hand, elbow on her desk, as she studied George Johnson's tax documents on her large screen monitor. The Johnsons seemed to own half the businesses in Prescott and there were almost as many Johnsons as there were McBrides.

The thought of the McBrides once again brought Blake to mind. He'd been on her mind a lot since she's seen him on Saturday. So many times she'd started to look for that list of 4-H'ers with Blake and Demi's phone number on it but something had stopped her.

She wasn't sure what that something was. Maybe it was the pain she'd been through since the last time she'd seen him.

If he was still angry with her for what she'd done all those years ago, he hadn't shown it. Had it been pity that stayed his anger? The scar across her face and her altered features could have taken away whatever fury he might feel at the way she'd left him.

Cat grabbed her mug, got up from her seat, and walked out of her office toward the break room to pour herself another cup of coffee. The smell of coffee was strong in the room as she entered, and she breathed the scent in. She filled her mug from the carafe before setting it back on the warmer. After dumping plenty of creamer and sugar in her coffee and stirring it with a spoon, she went to the sink and rinsed off the spoon. Then she turned off the warmer and washed the coffee pot. She would be the last to leave and needed to leave everything clean for tomorrow.

Without meaning to, she glanced at the mirror over the sink and paused. After all of this time since she'd been given a new face and had borne the scar, she still couldn't get used to seeing herself in the mirror. She knew she wasn't ugly...she just wasn't *her* anymore. The scar detracted from whatever beauty the plastic surgeon might have given her. Her nose was smaller, her lips a little fuller, her cheekbones not quite so high.

One thing she did still have, was a dimple when she smiled, and of course her golden-brown eyes were still large with dark lashes framing them. A dimple and golden eyes were all that remained of her former appearance.

The scar...that was the hardest to look at. Life had changed for her and she'd seldom dated after the accident.

A couple of years after the accident, she had married Eddie and they'd had Melanie. Things were fine at the start, but had eventually turned rocky, especially when he'd started to drink. It was a couple of beers here and there, but it had hit Cat hard since both of her parents had been alcoholics.

After Melanie died, any connection she and Eddie had shared was gone.

She'd had other relationships, but none of them had been serious. It was like she'd lost the ability to truly love anyone after Blake.

Despite what she'd been through with Eddie, she'd had Melanie. That had been what really mattered, so she couldn't regret Eddie.

As far as relationships since her divorce were concerned, had she really given anyone else a chance? If she was honest with herself, she'd closed herself off, hiding behind the scar and pain of past failed relationships.

With a sigh, she turned away from the mirror, carrying her coffee mug back to her desk. Cat had been hired because one of the CPAs, the Hartford of Hartford and Lake, had retired. She was still working through his client list, familiarizing herself with the clients he'd been working with. She'd made it through the J's so far.

Another accountant and a receptionist worked in the office along with the CPA, but they'd already left for the day and Cat was alone with her client records and her thoughts. She sat at her desk and scooted her chair up as she set the mug on her desk.

Since she'd arrived back in Prescott permanently to care for her grandmother, no one had recognized Cat. She was fine with that. She'd run into a couple of people she'd known and had to reintroduce herself. One of them was Karla Jennings who had convinced her to take on the horse club.

Over the past few years, Cat had only popped into town on weekends here and there to see her grandmother, then left before she could run into anyone she'd known from the past. The town was big enough that she could arrive and leave without questions.

Where once she'd been considered to have a sparkling personality and had been called a social butterfly by some folks, Cat was now a little more reserved and kept to herself. She'd probably make friends easier if she let herself go again.

Her so-called sparkling personality had been partly real and partly a façade to cover her true emotions. With a physically abusive and alcoholic father and an alcoholic mother, there hadn't been a lot to smile about at home. Away from her parents' house, Cat could be someone else entirely. She could be the girl she was meant to be.

When her mother had died, things had worsened with her father and he'd become more and more violent. Grandmother Hayden stepped in and took Cat in as a teenager and her life had improved. Her grandmother was a strict but loving woman. The fact that she was so ill now made Cat heartsick.

The only one who had ever known what Cat had been through with her father and mother was Blake. When she'd shared her secrets with him, he'd wanted to go straight to her house and beat the shit out of her father. She'd had to beg Blake to drop it. It had been all she could do to stop him.

A loud ringing jerked her out of her thoughts, startling her, and she realized it was the office phone. She took a deep breath as she brought herself to the present.

"Hartford and Lake," she answered.

It was one of James Lake's clients and she jotted down the person's name and phone number and disconnected from the call.

As she hung up, her cell phone rang and she checked the

display to see that it was Grandma Hayden.

Cat put a smile in her voice. "Hi, Grandma."

"Hello, sweetheart." The elderly woman's voice held only a hint of a waver despite the illness eating away at her.

"Need me at your house?" Cat did her best not to show the concern she felt. Her grandmother didn't like worry or pity, a trait shared by her granddaughter.

"I just want you to pick up a few things at the grocery store, if you can," Grandma Hayden said.

"No problem." Cat grabbed a sticky note with the accounting firm's name on it. "What do you need?"

Grandma named a few things that Cat scratched down on the notepaper.

"Got it." She put down the pen she was holding. "See you when I stop by."

For years, Cat's cousin, Margo, had cared for Grandma, but Margo had passed away from a heart attack a couple of months ago. Their grandmother had refused to go to a retirement home and, despite what Grandma Hayden said, the elderly woman needed someone to check in on her periodically and make sure she was all right. As far as Cat was concerned, it should be family. Grandma Hayden had all but raised her and Cat wanted to be there for her.

Cat went back to working on George's documents. She liked numbers. Liked how neat and orderly they were in comparison to her life, which had always seemed out of control.

Her thoughts flashed back to being in math class with Blake. She'd always excelled at math and would get an A to Blake's B every semester. Grades were a form of competition between them from the time they'd started high school. He beat her in Spanish and biology but she had him in math and English. They'd both been in FFA, studying agricultural education, and were usually in a dead tie there. They'd graduated in the top ten of their class.

Warmth flushed through her as she thought about how good Blake had looked. He'd always been muscular with a great body, but damn, he was even hotter now than he had been then. He'd filled out in a hard, sexy way that had made her heart race and her body tingle from head to toe. Through his shirt, it had almost looked like his muscles had muscles. The thought caused a giggle to rise up inside her.

She'd known she'd run into Blake sooner or later, she just hadn't expected to have the kind of reaction that she'd had. And she certainly hadn't expected to be obsessing about him.

In front of her, the screen blurred. She bit her lower lip and tried to turn her attention back to her work.

When her thoughts kept returning to Blake, she groaned and put her head on her arms in front of the keyboard. What would her life be like now if she'd never left Blake or Prescott?

It didn't do any good to think that way.

She finally gave up trying to concentrate on her accounting work, shut down her computer, and took her coffee mug to the kitchen to rinse it out. She grabbed her purse, headed for the front entrance, and locked it behind her.

Humming to herself, she got into her truck and soon was on her way to her grandmother's favorite grocery store.

She passed the local swimming pool and waves of memories washed over her. She'd had a summer job as a lifeguard and Blake would meet her there. Sometimes they'd go swimming and she remembered laughing with her friends, water fights with Blake, and stealing kisses in the deep end of the pool.

Often, after she got off work, they'd go out for pizza or play miniature golf, or go to the arcade. She couldn't help a smile at the thought of the things they'd done together.

The whole town was filled with memories. It seemed that everywhere she turned, something evoked thoughts of the past. Every now and then she would find herself wishing things had been different and that she'd made different choices, but then chided herself. She was lucky to be alive and to be healthy and relatively whole. The scar reminded her of that every day when she looked at herself in the mirror.

It was Monday afternoon and the grocery store wasn't too crowded. Cat pushed her basket up and down the aisles, picking out things for herself and for her grandmother. Cat had never been crazy about cooking and living on her own gave her the excuse to make fast and easy meals. She figured she wouldn't make the best cook if she ever did get married, but she could nuke a mean ready-made dinner and she could dial the phone with the best of them to get carryout from her favorite restaurants.

She did, however, love fruit and fresh vegetables and her hamster, Sam, appreciated them too, especially apple chunks. She guided the cart to the produce section and immediately started gathering ingredients for salsa, which included plum tomatoes, garlic, jalapeños, a habanero pepper, onions, and limes.

Just as she was twisting a tie on the bag of jalapeños, she looked up and saw a familiar face. She turned from her basket and looked at the woman she'd known since elementary school. "Jackie?"

The pretty blonde glanced from the carrots to Cat. "Yes,"

Jackie said. "Do I know you?"

Cat moved closer. "Cat Hayden."

"Cat?" Jackie looked surprised and set down the bunch of carrots she'd picked up. "Is that really you?"

With a smile, Cat nodded.

Jackie reached out and hugged Cat who hugged her friend in return. Jackie stepped back. "It's hard to believe it's you. You don't look anything like I remember."

"Long story," Cat said. "I was in an accident with a horse and had to have reconstructive surgery." She was tired of having to explain herself every time she ran into someone she knew from the past, but there wasn't much she could do about it without taping the explanation to her forehead.

Jackie's eyes widened. "I'm so sorry."

Cat gave a casual shrug. "It was a long time ago. Not too long after I left Prescott."

"With Toby Jennings," Jackie said.

Cat sighed. "The biggest mistake of my life. Getting stomped on by a horse was a close second."

"That bad, huh?" Jackie glanced at Cat's shopping basket. "Are you here to stay?"

Cat set her bag of jalapeños in the cart. "I just moved back three months ago and I don't plan on leaving."

"Three months?" Jackie put her hands on her hips. "And you haven't called me yet?"

Blake had said the same thing.

With a sheepish smile, Cat said, "I planned to."

Jackie waved it off with a grin. "We need to go out for coffee. Or better yet, a drink after work sometime." Jackie pulled her cell phone out of her purse. "Give me your number and I'll call you."

Cat gave her number to Jackie who put it into her contacts. When she finished, Jackie asked, hesitantly, "Have you talked with Blake?"

The sound of Blake's name sent a burst of warmth through Cat, followed by a wistfulness she'd never expected. With a not-so-casual shrug, she tried to sound indifferent as she said, "I saw him Saturday."

Jackie's tone was hopeful. "Did you go out with him?"

Cat found herself wishing they had as she shook her head. "His daughter is in the 4-H horse club that I'm working with now. I saw him when he picked her up."

"Oh." Jackie sounded disappointed. "What did he have to say?"

"Not much." Cat put a smile on her face. "I told him what a great rider his daughter is. She's a better barrel racer than I was at her age."

Jackie raised her brows. "Considering all of the trophies you racked up over the years, that's pretty damned good."

Cat nodded. "I think she's a little star."

"I'd better get going." Jackie gave Cat another hug. "I'll call you. We have lots to catch up on."

"Yes, we do," Cat said when they parted. "Lots."

Cat finished her shopping and tried not to think about the way Jackie had studied her, obviously unable to keep from looking at the scar. It was always that way whether she was first meeting a person or had run into someone she'd known before the accident.

After she paid for the groceries, she pushed her cart out to the parking lot and loaded her groceries into the passenger seat of her truck and headed to her grandma's. Considering each of them lived alone, there weren't a lot of groceries to load.

Despite her illness, Grandma Hayden had insisted on Cat having her own place rather than moving in with her grandmother like she'd offered to. Grandma had said that Cat needed her freedom. Cat had relented and found a house around the corner from her grandma's so she could be there in no time if the elderly woman needed her.

When she arrived at Grandma Hayden's, Cat carried in the groceries after unlocking the door using the key she'd been given.

She tucked her keys into her pocket. "Hi, Grandma," she called out as she took everything to the small kitchen.

Her grandma was in the pantry. Her petite figure was wasting away to nothing, making Cat heartsick. Grandma had always been stout and larger than life, and it was hard to see her this way.

Grandma Hayden turned around. For a moment Cat thought she saw pain flash across her grandmother's face, but that was replaced with a smile.

"Thank you, Catharine," she said as she looked at the bags Cat had just set on the table with noisy thumps.

"It was no problem." Cat went to her grandma and hugged her. She smelled of lavender sachet and felt small and frail in Cat's arms. When she drew away, she said, "I can't stay long. I have groceries in the car that I need to take home and get into the fridge."

"Supper on Sunday?" Her grandmother asked as she took a carton of eggs out of one of the bags.

"You know I wouldn't miss it." Cat put a container of rainbow sherbet, her grandmother's favorite, into the freezer.

"Good." Grandma Hayden returned to the bags and took out

a quart of milk. "I'm making fried chicken, green beans, mashed potatoes, and gravy. Apple crumble is for dessert."

"Yum." Cat put her hand to her belly. "You know I love your fried chicken, no matter how bad it is for me."

Grandma Hayden laughed. "Sweetie, I've been eating fried foods all my life, going on eighty-five years now, and I've done just fine."

"Yes, you have." Cat folded up the now empty plastic grocery bags and tucked them into the pantry. "Don't worry, Grandma. Nothing will stop me from eating your fried chicken." She smiled. "Just talking about it is making me hungry for it right now." She turned back from the pantry. "I ran into Jackie Dunham at the grocery store."

"How's that girl doing?" Grandma Hayden asked. "What's she been up to?"

"She looks great." Cat thought about the pretty blonde. "Of course, she didn't recognize me." She stuffed her hand into her pocket and grasped her keys, which jingled when she pulled them out. "But we're going out for coffee or a drink to catch up. She's going to call me."

"Good." Grandma Hayden smiled. "You need to get out of that house more."

Cat nodded. "I think you're right." She gave her grandmother a quick kiss on the cheek. "I'd better get those groceries home. I'll see you on Sunday."

"See you then, Catharine," the elderly woman said.

As Cat started out of the room she looked over her shoulder. "Call me if you need anything before then."

"Don't you worry about me," Grandma Hayden said. "I'll be

just fine."

Cat gave her grandmother a little wave before she headed out the front door, locking it behind herself. As she jogged down the porch steps toward her car, memories came back to her of the times Blake had been waiting for her at the bottom of the stairs, a sexy smile on his rough features. He'd always had a rough look about him, even when he was young. She'd loved the way he looked as well as the way he held himself, his easy stride, and his natural confidence.

She reached the last step and paused, thinking about the way he would kiss her while she stood on the bottom step, bringing her to eye level with him. His kisses never failed to set her on fire.

Why had she left him? After the fight they'd had, she'd ended up becoming infatuated with Toby Jennings for all of the wrong reasons. Choosing Blake meant staying in a town filled with bad memories of her abusive father. Toby meant getting away from Prescott and into the wide world just waiting for her.

Nothing had turned out the way she'd thought it would. Nothing.

CHAPTER 3

Cat Hayden. Her name went through Blake's mind once again. KitCat was back.

A breeze tugged at his work shirt as he rested his hands on the top wood rail of the riding arena and stared out at the valley. A mix of emotions clenched his gut. Twisted inside him was a good dose of anger at the way she'd left him, surprise at how the accident had changed the way she looked, and an uncertain feeling about the fact that she'd returned.

Part of him knew that they'd both been young and he shouldn't hold what had happened against her. Hell, they'd both been only eighteen, not more than kids. But the other part of him couldn't get past the fact she hadn't even said goodbye.

He gripped his leather gloves in one hand and tugged down

his Stetson with the other, shading his eyes from the warm Arizona sun.

When he'd hugged her, memories had flooded him, one after another. She had the same soft scent that he remembered and he'd breathed her in without even realizing he was doing so. She had felt good in his arms, familiar and comfortable, even for the short time he'd held her.

She'd looked so different but her eyes were the same beautiful golden-brown and she still had that dimple when she smiled as she was complimenting his daughter's abilities.

His heart had known it was Cat even before she'd told him. Nineteen years and a new face couldn't take that knowledge away from him.

Her quieter, less confident attitude had taken him aback. She'd always been confident and outgoing. She seemed more reserved now, guarded even. He'd noticed how she'd put her hand up to her face as they talked, as if embarrassed by the way she looked. He didn't give a damn about the scar and he hated the way it seemed to make her feel about herself.

She must have been through hell and back once that horse had tried to kill her. He couldn't imagine the kind of pain she'd been through, both physically and emotionally.

Damn, but he'd loved her and she'd broken his heart and scattered the shards across the valley. He'd known she wanted to get away from Prescott, but he'd never expected her to leave like she did.

In some ways it reminded him of Sally... His ex-wife had always battled drug and alcohol addiction and had gone through rehab before abandoning her husband and daughter to run off with a man she'd met in rehab. Blake had never loved Sally—the only reason they'd married was out of duty, because he'd gotten her pregnant. They'd only dated a few times and then a month later she'd come to him, telling him that she was having his child.

The single good thing to come out of that marriage was Demi. And that girl meant everything to him.

Despite the fact that he hadn't loved Sally, it had still stung when she'd left him and Demi. The hardest part was telling his daughter that Sally wasn't coming back and then seeing how much it had devastated Demi to lose her mother.

That had been eight years ago, when Demi was six.

Blake shook his head. Hell, it wasn't fair to compare Cat and Sally. The situations had been different, and the women couldn't be more different. Cat had left after they had broken up over the fact that he wouldn't leave Prescott and she couldn't wait to escape their small town.

But he couldn't help but feel guarded after what had happened with each of the two women.

He pushed away from the wooden fence rail and tucked his work gloves into his back pocket, then walked around the barn so that he could see his sprawling ranch house. An unfamiliar truck was parked in front of the house. Whoever it was must have driven up while Blake had been out riding the range.

When he reached the house, he jogged up the porch stairs then wiped his boots on the rubber mat in front of the door before entering. It was cool inside with no sign of Demi, or anyone else, for that matter. He frowned.

He walked through the house to Demi's room. Maybe one of her friends had come over. Although, considering she was only fourteen, she didn't have any friends who could drive themselves anywhere.

When he reached her room, her door was closed but he heard voices from the other side. Demi's voice and another that definitely wasn't female.

He grabbed the doorknob and opened the door. Demi was cross-legged on the bed and a good-looking teenage boy was sitting close to her. In one sweep of his gaze, Blake saw books and papers scattered on the comforter... And he saw the way the boy was looking at his daughter.

The boy and Demi looked up. A look of fear crossed the boy's face.

Jaw clenched, Blake strode over to the boy, grabbed him by the collar, and jerked him to his feet.

"Dad!" Demi slid off the bed, horror on her face. "What are you doing? Stop it!"

"What the hell are you doing in here with my daughter?" Blake said in a growl as he jerked the boy out of the bedroom.

The boy looked terrified. "We were just—"

"Shut up." Anger made Blake's gut burn as he marched the boy toward the front door.

"Dad!" Demi hurried beside him. "Stop it! Let Brett go! We were studying. What are you doing?"

Blake flung open the front door and shoved Brett onto the porch. "I don't want to ever see you around my daughter again."

He cut his gaze to Demi. "Get his things."

Demi had her hands clenched into fists at her sides. She whirled around and ran toward her room.

Blake turned his glare on Brett. "How old are you?"

Brett's throat worked as he swallowed. "Sixteen."

"My daughter is fourteen years old," Blake growled. "You have no business being around her."

The boy looked frantic. "I was tutoring—"

"I don't want to hear a word out of you," Blake said in a growl.

Brett clamped his mouth shut.

"Here." Tears wavered in Demi's voice as she came up beside Blake and pushed a backpack at him.

Blake, in turn, shoved the backpack into the boy's arms. "Get on out of here and don't ever come back into my home again."

Brett didn't hesitate. He grabbed the backpack, turned and jogged down the stairs, and headed toward his truck. He didn't look back as he got into his truck. Moments later the truck tore down the dirt road, dust roiling up from the tires.

"How could you?" Demi shouted and Blake turned to face her. "How could you embarrass me like that?"

"Get to your room." Blake narrowed his gaze. "We'll talk about this when you calm down."

"Calm down?" Her fists were still clenched at her sides, her eyes glossy with tears. "You were the one who overreacted and threw my friend out for no reason."

"Friend?" Blake nearly roared the word. "You're fourteen and you had a sixteen-year-old boy in your room. Boys that age have only one thing in mind and it sure as hell isn't studying."

"Brett's not like that," Demi shouted. "He's a nice guy."

"Get on out of here and go to your room," he repeated.

"I hate you!" Demi stamped her foot, tears rolling down her face now. "I wish Mom was here. She wouldn't have embarrassed me."

The words hit Blake like a concrete block to his chest. He pointed to the hallway. "To your room. *Now.*"

Demi looked like she wanted to say something else but she spun and ran away from him, and then disappeared down the hallway. A moment later a door slammed.

Blake stared in the direction his daughter had gone. A slow burn in his chest threatened to erupt as he thought about the boy being alone with his daughter in her room and he gritted his teeth.

He raised his hat and pushed his hand through his hair before settling his hat on his head again. Had he overreacted?

Hell, no. That boy had no damned business being anywhere near his daughter.

The sound of a truck coming up the drive caught his attention. "It had better not be that boy," Blake growled out loud.

With his jaw clenched, he headed back outside to see his brother's truck coming up to the house, the truck pulling a horse trailer. Gage parked and climbed out of his vehicle and adjusted his straw Stetson on his head.

"What's gone and ticked you off?" Gage asked as Blake met him at the foot of the stairs.

Blake scowled. "Damned sixteen-year-old boy was in Demi's room with her when I got home."

"And you chased him off with a shotgun," Gage stated as if he knew it was fact.

Blake's eyes were narrowed. "Boy had no business being around my daughter."

"I bet Demi didn't take that too well," Gage said.

"Sent her to her room." Blake set his jaw.

Gage eyed Blake steadily. "She's a good kid, Blake. You know that."

"Yeah, she's a helluva good kid." Blake let out his breath. "I just don't want her to end up like her mother."

"You can't come unhinged on her like that," Gage said. "She might start doing things she shouldn't out of sheer rebellion. You know how kids are. Hell, you were one yourself if you can't remember that far back."

Blake thought about what Demi had said—that she wished her mother were here. He felt another blow to his heart. Was he being too hard on her? Was she getting the feminine influence that she needed?

He looked away from his brother, at the land stretched out before him. When Blake looked back at Gage, he said, "So why did you stop by?"

"You must be getting old, big brother," Gage said, with an amused smile. "I came over to see that young bull of yours."

Well, hell. He'd forgotten that. Maybe he was getting old.

Gage drove away with the young Angus bull loaded into the horse trailer, and Blake headed back into the house. He'd thought long and hard about it, and maybe he hadn't handled the whole situation well.

He closed the front door behind him and went to Demi's room. When she'd entered her teens, he'd started knocking on her door before he let himself in. This time he knocked and waited for her to answer.

Silence followed and he knocked again. "Demi, we need to have a talk."

Still nothing but silence. He tried the knob but it was locked.

He braced his hand on the doorframe. "You'd better open this door now if you don't want me to take the whole thing off its hinges."

A moment passed before heard the lock click. The knob turned and the door opened about an inch and stopped. He pushed the door open and walked into her room. He stopped and studied his daughter who was on the bed doing her homework, her head bent over a math book and her long blonde hair falling across her face so that he couldn't see her eyes. Her cell phone was on the bed beside her thigh.

He gave an inward sigh and moved to her bed. The bedsprings squeaked and the mattress dipped under his weight as he sat on the edge of the four-poster bed. The canopy and her comforter were white with tiny purple flowers. Her room was done in purple with posters of horses and a collection of horse figurines on a shelf that went along one long wall.

She refused to look at him, just kept doing her math homework. For some reason that reminded him of Cat and how they'd studied together and how she'd always kicked his ass in math. But he and Cat had been the same age-—although that hadn't stopped him from thinking about sex every time he was around her.

"Demi." His voice sounded gruff and he cleared his throat as he tried to even his tone. "We need to talk."

She ignored him, but her pencil faltered a little.

"Look at me," he said, but she didn't look up. He repeated, more firmly this time. "Look at me."

She set down her pencil, leaving it on her math book, and slowly raised her head. Her eyes were red and he could tell she'd been crying.

But she had a hard set to her jaw that told him how angry she was. It reminded him a lot of himself at her age.

"Maybe I didn't handle that in the best way," he started.

"You think?" she said, in a sarcastic tone.

"But you know the rules," he continued. "No boys in your room. You're fourteen and a sixteen-year-old boy has no business in your bedroom. Hell, no teenage boy of any age belongs in your room."

"We were just studying." She glared at him. "We weren't doing anything wrong. Besides he's not like that—he wouldn't do anything. He didn't do anything wrong."

"I was his age once," Blake said. "And I damned sure know how teenage boys think."

"He's not like you," she snapped back.

"Honey, all teenage boys have one thing on their minds." Blake tapped her math book. "And it's not homework."

She raised her chin. "I can't believe you don't trust me and that you treated him like that."

"I made that rule for a reason." Blake studied her for a long moment. "It's boys. I don't trust boys."

Her tone grew sharper. "If you trusted me, you would never have done what you did."

"It had nothing to do with trusting you," he said. They were going around in circles. "It has everything to do with boys being boys."

"You embarrassed me." Her bottom lip trembled. "How could you do that? I'm not going to be able to show my face at school."

As he studied his daughter, Blake wondered if he was enough for her. Maybe she needed a feminine touch or support from a woman who wouldn't go crazy when she talked about boys and dating.

Blake let out a sigh. "I'm sorry, Demi. You're right. I should have handled it differently, but I didn't. But you need to follow the rules. No boys are allowed in your bedroom."

"I want to go live with Mom." Demi crossed her arms over her chest and the set of her jaw reminded him of himself. "She's not as strict as you are and she wouldn't have that stupid rule."

Again, pain slammed into his chest. Demi knew exactly what she was doing when she'd said she wanted to live with Sally.

"That's not going to happen." He kept his tone even. "I have full custody and it's going to stay that way."

"Why?" Her glare was back. "Mom has an apartment now, someplace that I can live."

It was true that Sally wasn't transient any longer, but knowing Sally, her life could turn from stable to unstable at any moment. Once again she could turn back to drugs and alcohol if she hadn't already, and he wasn't about to allow his daughter to be put in that kind of situation. Sally was the one he didn't trust one damned bit.

Blake tried to relax because his body had tensed at the thought of Sally.

"I was very clear about it before," Blake said, "I need you to follow the rules of this house. Boys aren't allowed in your bedroom. Period."

"That's not fair." She grabbed an old stuffed horse and held it tightly to her chest like she had as a young girl. Ironically, she added, "You treat me like a little girl."

"You're a young woman now and not a little girl," he said. "But we have rules in this house and that's just how it's going to be. You know there are consequences to breaking the rules. If I find you with that boy again, you'll lose your cell phone for a week."

She looked at him stubbornly. "That's not fair."

"If you follow the rules then you don't have to worry about losing privileges," he said. "But when you don't follow them, there will be consequences for your actions."

Her jaw was set and she scowled.

"You're growing up to be a beautiful young woman," Blake added quietly. "I want you to know how proud I am of you."

Demi said nothing but looked away. She was a lot like he'd been as a teenager and he knew it was hard to back down once riled up.

He touched the side of her face and brought her back to face him. "I love you. Always remember that."

She looked down at the stuffed horse she was holding and he let his hand fall away from her face.

"I'm going to fix dinner now." He stood and the bedsprings creaked again. "How do tacos sound?"

Even though he knew tacos were her favorite meal, she shrugged.

"I'll let you know when dinner's ready," he said before walking out of her bedroom and closing the door behind him.

CHAPTER 4

Thunder rolled across the valley and rattled the barn and Cat scooted closer to Blake on the alfalfa hay bale they were both sitting on. Rain pattered against the wood as the storm went on but the barn was well built and no water leaked through any cracks.

It was Cat's eighteenth birthday and they'd spent the day together, going to a movie followed by eating at the local pizza place where all of the seniors hung out. What a perfect way to end the day, alone with Blake, feeling like they were shut away from the world.

She leaned her head against him and he put his arm around her shoulders and held her close.

"You're not afraid of thunderstorms," he said in a teasing voice.

She tilted her face to look up at him. "No, but it's a good excuse to snuggle next to you."

He gave her a sexy little grin. "You don't need an excuse to cuddle with me." He lowered his head slowly and brought his mouth to hers.

Blake could kiss like no other guy she'd ever been with. Not that there had been a lot of guys, but he seemed like he had a world's worth of experience, despite the fact that he was the same age as she was, now that she was eighteen, too.

His kiss was slow and gentle but deepened with the kind of passion she'd been feeling for a long time with him. Unfulfilled passion.

He raised his head and his voice was husky when he spoke. "I want to give your birthday present to you now."

She felt a little shiver run through her at the way he was looking at her. "You've shown me a fantastic birthday," she said. "You don't need to give me anything."

He stood, grasped her hand, and pulled her to her feet. "Come on. I want somewhere private to give it to you where we won't be disturbed if one of my brothers decides to come out here."

She smiled and he continued to hold her hand as he led her to the ladder that went up to the hayloft. He let her go first and she could sense him watching her butt as she climbed up. She wiggled it a little just to give him a bit of a show. He was definitely an ass man.

"Did I ever tell you what great ass-ets you have?" he said from below.

She glanced over her shoulder and smiled. "Many times."

He gave a low laugh. "It doesn't hurt to say it again."

When she reached the top, she flung herself onto a pile of hay, laughing as the yellow straw fell onto her face. It poked through her blouse and chafed her belly where her blouse had hiked up. Her short jean skirt had also moved up to the top of her thighs, and she tugged it down. Just a little.

She looked up when she heard Blake's bootsteps and then he was looking down at her and smiling. She scooted up and he eased down beside her and he brushed straw from her hair before they both leaned back against the hay.

Thunder boomed, the sound loud to her ears. The barn lights flickered.

"The power might go out," she murmured against his lips.

"Now, that would be a shame." He kissed her then drew back before he shoved his hand into his pocket and pulled out a thin gold foil box with a gold bow wrapped around it.

Her eyes widened and she looked up at him. "You'd better not have spent too much money on me, Blake McBride."

He grinned. "Just open it, little Cat."

She bit her lower lip as she took the box from him. She felt the swirled pattern on the foil against her fingertips as she held it and then she pulled at the gold bow wrapped around the box. The bow fell into her lap. She hesitated as she put her hand on the box's lid. Her eyes met his and she saw a world of emotions in his gaze.

The lid opened easily and she caught her breath. Nestled in a bed of white satin was a fine gold bracelet. The bracelet was made with two slender bangles connected by a heart at the top, and by a gold chain at the bottom.

"I love it, Blake." Warmth flowed through her heart as she looked up at him. "It's beautiful."

"Read the inscription." He took the bracelet out of the box and held it in his palm. His hand was so big and the bracelet looked small and delicate against it.

Her breathing was fast as she looked at the beautiful gift he had given her. Inside, the inscription read, "You'll always be my little KitCat. Love, Blake."

She smiled up at him. "Thank you."

He clasped it on her wrist. "That's so you'll never forget that I love you."

"You know how much I love you, too." She wrapped her arms around his neck and kissed him. It was a kiss filled with everything she felt for Blake. It was more than love. It was more than caring. It was a deep friendship between two people who loved each other so much that it could never be taken away.

The box and ribbon scattered on the floor of the loft as she rolled onto her back in the hay and he rolled on top of her. His weight felt comfortable, like he belonged there, his narrow hips between her thighs.

They had never made love even though it was clear that they'd wanted each other for a long time. Maybe they were just waiting for the right moment. Or maybe he had been waiting until she was eighteen.

Regardless, none of it mattered. He was all hers and she wanted him in every way possible.

Lightning crashed and heavy rain pounded the barn roof as Blake kissed her and touched her gently in all the right places. He caused her to sigh and moan and cry out. He drove her crazy with the want and need that had been building inside her for so very long.

A frenzy of need took hold of her and she arched up to him as he slid between her thighs—

Cat sat up in bed, her heart pounding and aching all at once.

She felt unfulfilled and her belly clenched with longing.

She hadn't had that dream in so long… When she'd left Blake, the dream and her mistake had haunted her for years. Over time, the dream had faded. She should have known it would come back once she saw him again. She'd thought her heart was healed, but this just proved that nineteen years hadn't been anywhere near enough time away from him.

She pushed the covers aside, slid out of bed, and went to her antique wood jewelry box. She was surprised to realize that her hands were shaking a little as she reached into the hidden pocket at the back. Her fingers touched cool metal and she drew out the gold bracelet that Blake had given her for her eighteenth birthday… The stormy night she'd lost her virginity to the man she loved.

That night they hadn't been kids anymore. They'd been a man and a woman in love.

The fight had come six months later, and then she'd gone and thrown it all away.

She hadn't looked at the bracelet for nineteen years. It was a wonder she even remembered she had it. She turned the bracelet so that it caught the light and she could see the inscription on the back.

You'll always be my little KitCat. Love, Blake.

A tear almost made its way to her eye but she managed to hold it back. *Damn. Damn, damn, damn.* She was thirty seven years old now, too old to be sick over lost young love.

She slipped the gold bracelet back into its secret pocket and closed the jewelry box. Even though a part of her wanted to cry for that lost love, the other part of her knew that it was useless. It had been a long time ago. Whatever love had been there was long gone, and there was nothing to cry over any more.

She pushed her fingers through her hair and wandered into the living room and went up to Sam's cage.

"Been up all night?" Cat bent and peeked into the extravagant habitat to see Sam curled up in his nest.

At least he was in the habitat and not running around the house. If she could only figure out how he got out and then managed to get back in. He'd explore the house at night, wandering around and searching for treasures to pack into his cheeks. When he'd return she'd discover things in his nest like missing earrings, beads, and other things that he'd found.

Sam peeked one eye open. When he saw her, he got up and put his paws and nose up against the clear plastic that separated them.

"You want a treat, huh?" Cat tapped the wall and the hamster's nose wriggled as he followed her finger. "I'll get you a piece of apple."

She headed to the kitchen. Hamsters were so much simpler than men.

* * * * *

Cat checked out the numbers on her desktop computer as she worked through a client's mess of a file. Mrs. Karchner needed a new bookkeeper in her office who knew what she was doing.

With a shake of her head she got up from her desk, and walked out of her office to the file cabinet beside Janie's desk. The receptionist was away from the office. Cat opened the third drawer down and searched the K's for Karchner.

Early morning spring air swirled into the office as someone

opened the entrance into the accounting firm's office. Cat glanced over her shoulder and her lips parted. Her heart beat a little faster.

It was Blake, and he'd never looked so good. He wore a black Stetson that he took off as he closed the door behind him and his hair was short and dark. A light blue shirt stretched across his broad chest, his sleeves rolled up and showing his large biceps. His Wranglers molded his muscular thighs and he wore a wide brown leather belt with a silver and gold buckle. The light stubble on his jaws gave him even more of a rugged look.

Seeing him brought back the dream of the first time they'd made love and her body tingled at the memory.

He swept his gaze across the room and his green eyes rested on her. A flicker of surprise registered across his expression.

"Hi, Blake." Marsha Solara, the other accountant, stood in the doorway to her office. She stirred her coffee. "What brings you here?"

Blake looked from Cat to Marsha. "Jim Hartford said he had a new accountant taking over my account now that he's retired." He raised an envelope. "Got a notice from the IRS that I need to discuss."

Marsha gave a nod toward Cat. "Blake, meet Cat Hayden, your new accountant. Cat, meet Blake McBride, your new client."

Cat's eyes widened. Blake was one of her new accounts?

Blake's gaze met hers again and neither one of them said anything.

Marsha cocked her head to the side. "You two already know each other?"

Cat nodded and Blake glanced back at Marsha. "We're acquainted," Blake said.

"Well, good." Marsha gave a thoughtful smile. "Cat, if you need anything, let me know."

"I will." Cat managed a smile and gestured to her office. "Come on in, Blake. I'll pull your file and be right there."

He gave a nod and walked into her office as she moved to the drawer with the M's. Her mind went blank for a moment and she wondered what she was doing there. All she could think about was Blake. Then she realized she was supposed to pull his file. She went through the M's and grabbed the file with "McBride, Blake" on the tab.

Clutching the file tightly to her chest, she walked to her office door where Blake was standing, waiting for her. Heart pounding, she moved past him, around her desk, and sat in the leather chair. Blake lowered himself into one of the armed chairs in front of the desk. He loosely held his western hat in one hand.

"Hi, Blake," she said and rested his file on the desk in front of her, near her keyboard. Again, she wanted to touch her scar and hide it from him—as if that was possible.

"You always were good with numbers," Blake said. "But I never expected you to become an accountant. I thought you'd go into some field that would involve working with animals."

She gave a slight shrug. "In college I found I had an aptitude for accounting, so that's the path I decided to take." After the accident, things had changed and she'd shied away from working with animals. The extensive therapy she'd gone through and her nervousness around horses for a few years after the accident, had kept her from going down that path. Sometimes she regretted that she hadn't pursued another career. With a hesitant smile, she said, "May I see the letter?"

He leaned forward and handed an envelope to her. Their fingers touched and the dream came rushing back to her. An electrical charge went through her, as if he knew exactly what she'd dreamed last night. For a wild moment she thought that maybe he'd dreamed it, too. She swallowed and took the envelope before sliding the papers out and unfolding them.

She scanned the page with her gaze. "So, you're being audited." She set the papers on her desk and shook her head. "For the past two years. That's certainly no fun."

The corner of his mouth quirked into a smile. "That just might be the understatement of the year."

"I'm going to need to review your file and likely I'm going to need access to all of your records," she said. "Is everything at your ranch?"

He gave a slow nod. "You're welcome to come out and take a look at anything you need to."

"Right now my schedule is pretty open." She turned to her computer and pulled up her schedule then glanced at Blake. "We might as well take advantage of my clear calendar and get your audit taken care of. Is anytime this week good for you?"

"The next few days I've got a lot planned," he said. "Do you work Saturdays?"

"That's not a problem," she said. "Ten in the morning?" He nodded and she put him on the schedule.

When she finished, she looked at him to find him studying her. Heat flushed over her and her scar tingled. Was he looking at her scar and thinking about how different she looked now?

"Do you have plans for dinner?" he asked in his slow drawl.

"No," she said. He'd caught her off guard.

"Why don't you have dinner with me?" He continued studying her with his even gaze. "We can go to the Hummingbird."

She couldn't think of a single reason why not. "I've heard it's a good restaurant," she said. "I've never had the opportunity to go."

"Now's your chance." He drew his cell phone out of the holster at his side and checked the time, then put the phone away again. "I've got a couple of things to take care of. How about I pick you up around seven?"

"All right." She stood and he stood with her. "I'll be ready. My house isn't far from my grandmother's." She cleared her throat and gave him her address.

He gave a nod then turned and headed out of her office to the firm's front door. She looked at his broad shoulders and his nice ass—really nice ass—as he walked away from her. He glanced over his shoulder as he reached the entrance and she felt another rush of heat as he caught her staring at him. She hurried to sit down and look at the computer monitor but the screen only blurred when she stared at it.

After he left, she wondered if she had made a mistake saying yes. Just being around him brought back memories and old feelings. Feelings better off not being examined or explored.

CHAPTER 5

Blake frowned as he walked away from the accounting firm. Should he have asked Cat to dinner? He still felt the old pain and that pain was accompanied by a healthy dose of mistrust. The way she'd left… He never wanted to go through any of that again. She'd done it to him once and almost destroyed him. She could very well do it a second time.

It wasn't fair of him to think that way. They'd broken up, so it wasn't like she'd run off on him. He'd lost her before that.

He had three more stops to make before heading back to the ranch. He needed to make a deposit at the bank, stop at the hardware store, and purchase feed for his horses from Hatch's Feed and Tack.

As he took care of errands, his mind kept turning to Cat. She was a beautiful woman who didn't seem to smile enough anymore. What would it take for her to smile like she used to?

A few minutes before seven, Blake showed up on Cat's front porch and rang the doorbell. After a brief moment, she opened the door.

Soft light fell across her face and she looked so gorgeous it took his breath away. Her long black hair fell over her nearly bare shoulders—thin straps held up the slim black dress she wore. Her golden-brown eyes were as wide and beautiful as they'd always been. She looked different but she was the same KitCat he'd never stopped loving.

And that was the truth of it. He'd never stopped loving her.

Her expression looked a little nervous and wary as she grabbed her purse and headed out the door, joining him on the porch, and he wondered why she would feel nervous. It was as if past experiences had made her skittish. What had she been through since he'd last seen her, all those years ago?

"You look beautiful," he said with a smile as the warm yellow porch light haloed her.

"Thank you." The light of surprise was in her eyes as she looked up at him, like she wasn't used to being complimented and that made him want to frown. Instead, he asked her, "Ready?"

"I'm looking forward to it," she said as she locked the door behind her.

The evening was pleasant with a cool breeze and her heels clicked on the sidewalk as they headed out to his truck. They walked through the front gate of the white picket fence, the gate squeaking as it opened and closed. He helped her into the passenger's side and then walked around the truck and climbed into the driver's seat.

He drove the vehicle downtown, near the building where Cat worked, to the Hummingbird Restaurant. Locals called it simply the Hummingbird. The folks who owned the place had been the victims of a man determined to close down the restaurant, but the truth had come out and the Hummingbird had been saved. Unfortunately, not before the stress took its toll on the family.

It was a nice place that had once been simply a café, but had been renovated and expanded into a full restaurant, which now had a bar section called Nectars. When they reached the restaurant, Blake opened the door and let Cat go in front of him, then followed her inside.

"Hi, Blake." Tess, the hostess, greeted Cat and Blake with a smile.

"How are you doing, Tess?" Blake gave her a friendly kiss on the cheek.

The petite blonde held out her hand to Cat. "I'm Tess Grady. My family owns the Hummingbird."

Cat returned Tess's smile and took her hand. "I'm Cat Hayden." She glanced around the place as they released their grips. "You have a beautiful restaurant."

"Thanks." Tess nodded, her short blonde curls bouncing close to her cheeks. "The family has put a lot of work into the Hummingbird. Now, follow me." Tess showed Cat and Blake to a nice table in a dim corner. "The four-course fondue is our newest addition to the menu and it is incredible," Tess said. "I highly recommend it."

"We just might do that," Blake said as she handed each of

them a menu.

"Penny will be taking care of you tonight," Tess said. "You two have a great evening." She left to take care of the next couple who had just entered the restaurant.

"I love this place," Cat said as she looked around at the décor. "It has a wonderful ambiance." She returned her gaze to Blake. "How long has it been open?"

"About two years now," Blake said. "Ryan is marrying into the family. Tess's sister, Megan, is his fiancée."

"That's great." Cat smiled. "How are Ryan and your other brothers?"

"Good," Blake said. "Creed is a professional bull rider and is newly married, Ryan is of course engaged, and Tate and Gage seem to be staying out of trouble. For the most part."

"Your younger brothers always were a handful." Cat grinned as if thinking about memories of the McBride brothers when they were young. "But no more than you."

"You've got that right." Blake shook his head at the thought of some of the mischief and trouble that he and his four brothers had gotten into over the years. He opened his menu. "Hungry?"

"Very." Cat opened hers and it was quiet for a moment.

He watched her over the top of his menu and she raised her gaze and their eyes met for a long moment. Her cheeks turned pink and she looked back at her menu. She was so damned cute.

Blake scanned the specials. "What do you think of the fondue for two?"

When he met her gaze again she was smiling. "I'm all for it."

"Then, fondue it is." They set their menus aside as a server stopped by their table.

The young woman looked first at Blake. "How are you doing, Mr. McBride?"

"Very good, Penny." Amused, Blake said, "You know I prefer that you call me Blake."

Penny gave him an impish look. "I knew you far too long as Mr. McBride before I was old enough to call you Blake."

He grinned and gestured to Cat. "Penny, this is Cat Hayden."

"Hi." Penny smiled at Cat. "It's nice to meet you."

"Just don't call me ma'am," Cat said with a laugh.

Penny gave a quick grin. "Never." She glanced at Blake then Cat again. "What would you two like tonight to drink?"

Cat selected a chardonnay while Blake went with a Blue Moon and they ordered the four-course fondue for two.

It wasn't long before a server brought Cat's wine and Blake's beer. He took a swig from his bottle and she sipped from her glass.

He leaned back in his chair and studied her. She returned his gaze, the nervousness seemingly gone from her features.

"I don't even know where to start, KitCat." The name came out easily, as if no time had passed at all since he'd called her that so many years ago. "Maybe we should start with, when did you come back to Prescott?"

"Three months ago," she said.

He raised a brow. "And you didn't call me in all that time?"

She shrugged. "I wanted to, but I didn't know how."

He gave her an amused look. "It's called picking up a phone and dialing."

A smile tipped the corners of her mouth and then she sobered. "I didn't know how you'd feel about me contacting you out of the blue."

"Never wonder, Cat," he said softly. "Even before we were more, we were friends. You can always call me."

She looked at him with something like surprise. Her lips parted like she was going to say something but then she didn't. Their gazes met for a long moment and held.

"Here's your fondue appetizer." Penny's voice cut through the moment. "This is Jacob who will be helping me take care of you tonight."

Blake took his gaze from Cat and he nodded to the waitress who stepped aside as a young man put a fondue pot at the center of their table. A candle warmed the bottom of the pot. Jacob stepped back and Penny set a plate with cubes of three different kinds of bread beside the warmer.

"This fondue is made from a trio of cheeses along with scallions, sherry, and white wine," Penny said and gave them each a plate and a fondue fork.

"Looks good, Pen." Blake gave the cute young waitress a smile.

Penny glanced at his beer and Cat's wine. "Ready for another?"

"I will be in a few moments," Cat said as she picked up her glass for another sip.

"I'll be right back with more for each of you," Penny said. "Enjoy the fondue," she added before she left with Jacob.

For a few moments they concentrated on using the fondue forks to stab cubes of bread and swirl them in the fondue before attempting to eat the piece without it dropping off the fork.

Cat giggled as her first cheese-dipped cube tumbled off her fork and landed on the tablecloth. "I think I need some more practice."

He liked the sound of her giggle, it made him smile.

"This is terrific," Cat said after she finished eating a piece and ran her tongue along her lower lip to get at some of the sauce there.

Blake watched her tongue dart out and felt a stirring in his gut at the sight.

"It's pretty damned good," he said after chewing and swallowing his first bite.

She smiled and slipped another cheesy bread cube into her mouth.

They laughed and smiled, as not all of their attempts were successful and sometimes the bread cubes would fall back into the cheese fondue or onto their plates. Blake was just thankful he didn't have one roll down the front of his shirt and land in his lap.

The fondue pot and empty bread plate were taken away as the second course was served, a house salad with bleu cheese dressing.

Cat stayed on safe subjects, asking about his brothers and his parents along with several of his cousins.

"My family always loved you." The words came to him without reservation. "They'll be glad to see you again."

She was quiet for a moment. "Even after the way I left?"

He nodded. "They'll always care about you. They always have."

She took another drink from her second glass of wine then lowered her glass. "Your family is one of the things I missed about Prescott."

"And?" he said, laying out the question.

She seemed to blush. "Yes, I missed you, too."

He gave her a grin. "Of course you did."

She rolled her eyes. "Still as confident as ever."

A low chuckle rose up inside him. He put down his salad fork as their dinner fondue arrived. Jacob took away their salad plates then set the next fondue pot in front of them.

"This is our burgundy wine infused with fresh herbs and spices," Penny said as she put plates in front of them with pieces of raw shrimp, filet mignon, and chicken. She explained how long each would need to be cooked in the wine at the end of the fondue forks. The server also set different sauces in sectioned-off plates in front of each of them and explained which sauce was for each type of meat.

As they ate, they didn't lack for conversation. It felt easy and natural and he felt the old Cat coming round, the one who laughed and smiled easily as opposed to the more quiet and reserved Cat that she'd been since he'd first seen her at Folsom Ranch.

After she finished eating the entrée, she patted her belly. "I'm so full. I don't know if I can take in the fourth course, dessert."

"Do you mind talking about the horse that attacked you?" he asked.

She paused a moment and a shadow passed over her features. He almost wished he hadn't brought it up, but they needed to talk about it and get it out into the open.

With a shake of her head, she said, "I don't mind."

"How did it happen?" he asked.

She pushed her hair out of her face, slid her plate to the side and relaxed in her seat. Even though she looked different, her mannerisms and the way she spoke were the same. He'd always loved the sound of her voice.

A server cleared away the fondue pot and dishes.

When the server left, Cat took a deep breath. "When I left…"

"With Toby Jennings," Blake said evenly.

She nodded, looking a little embarrassed. "Toby and I went to

Tucson. I found a job rehabilitating horses with the owner of some stables on the east side of town. The owner's name was Woody." She tucked hair behind her ear again in a heart-wrenchingly familiar gesture. "Woody had a new gelding come in, Firestorm, and I took him out of his stall to start working with him. My biggest mistake was not waiting for Woody."

Blake watched Cat steadily as he waited for her to go on.

Her throat worked as she swallowed and it seemed that a shiver traveled over her skin. "The next thing I knew, Firestorm had knocked me down. He started stomping on me and shattered bones in my face and all over my body. I screamed and Woody heard and got the horse off of me before he managed to kill me." She shook her head. "I don't remember much after that."

"Damn." The horror of what Cat had been through swept over him. "I'm sorry, honey."

"It changed my life, that's for sure." She sighed. "Toby couldn't cope with it, especially the differences in my looks and the brain trauma. He couldn't handle all of the slow progress with this therapy and that. He took off for Wyoming last I heard."

"That sonofabitch," Blake growled.

She shrugged. "That was a long time ago."

"You suffered brain trauma?" he said.

She touched the side of her head and gave a crooked smile. "I can show you the scars. Brain surgery and everything."

"Do you have any problems left over from the trauma?" he asked.

"Other than the occasional nightmare or migraine, no," she said. "Although I do get a few aches and pains during rainy weather and my joints creak."

"Hell, my joints creak sometimes," he said with a grin. "Just don't tell my brothers or they're going to start calling me old man."

She returned his grin. "Can't imagine anyone calling you old man." She looked at the power in his body, his muscular frame. "You work out a lot, don't you?"

He nodded. "I run the hills around here and I have a weight set in a back room at the ranch. I started running and lifting when you left—it was a way to work out my frustrations. Eventually it became a way to relieve everyday stress."

The thought that he'd started lifting and running because of her made her wonder if that had been a good thing. The results had certainly been rewarding.

Their dessert arrived—a big fondue pot of pure dark chocolate along with plates of sliced fresh fruit that included strawberries, banana, and pineapple. There were also cubed pieces of brownies and golden pound cake.

"Oh, my." Cat closed her eyes and her chest rose as she inhaled and gave a happy sigh as she opened her eyes. "Smells heavenly and looks so good." She stabbed a strawberry with her fondue fork and twirled it in the chocolate.

"Sure does," Blake agreed, holding back his amusement at the enthusiastic way she greeted the dessert. He pierced a chunk of brownie with his own fork.

She drew her strawberry out of the chocolate fondue then plucked it off with her fingers. She closed her eyes again as she bit into the chocolate dipped strawberry. "Mmmmm…" She sounded and looked slightly orgasmic as she ate it.

His jaw tensed, an ache suddenly tightening his groin. Damn, that was hot.

She opened her eyes and caught him watching her. "What? Do I have chocolate on my face?"

He couldn't help a quick grin. "You look cute eating chocolate fondue."

She looked a little embarrassed and maybe a little shy. "Aren't you going to have some?"

"You bet." He dipped the brownie cube into the fondue then brought it out and popped it into his mouth. He chewed and swallowed then said, "That is good."

With a smile, she said, "This was a great idea."

He nodded. "We'll have to thank Tess."

Despite saying she was full earlier, she ate every piece of fruit, brownie, and cake on her plate and he did the same.

"That was so very good," she said and smiled as the server took the dessert fondue away.

Moments later, cups of coffee were brought to them to finish off their evening.

Blake set aside the last bottle of beer and took a drink of his coffee then set the cup down. He looked at her a long moment before he said, "Nineteen years ago the last thing I heard was that you were leaving town with Toby."

Cat looked down at her coffee cup and wouldn't meet his gaze for a long moment. When she finally looked at him again, she said, "It was probably the second biggest mistake of my life."

"What was the first?" Blake asked.

Her cheeks flushed. "The night we broke up... That was the worst night of my life and my biggest mistake."

A feeling of surprise caught him off guard and he had to ask his next question. "Why did you leave with him?"

Her throat worked as she swallowed. "You know why, Blake. It was the reason we broke up. I had to get away from Prescott and my father. I—I just couldn't live here anymore. You wouldn't leave this place behind because you wanted the land and your family more than you wanted me."

"You know that's not fair, Cat." He frowned. "I had a hell of a lot of responsibility here. And if you want to look at it that way, you wouldn't stay here for me."

She shrugged. "No one is to blame. At that time in our lives we each wanted different things."

"Sometimes I blame myself, though." His own admission surprised him. "If I had tried harder to keep you here, if I hadn't let us break up the way we did—"

"You couldn't have stopped me, Blake. I had to get away." Cat shook her head. "My father… Things just weren't good."

Blake clenched his jaw, remembering the things Cat had told him about her father. "I should have beat the shit out of him then."

Cat leaned forward. "No. Walking away was the right thing to do. I know you wanted to protect me, but by then I was with my grandmother and he couldn't hurt me anymore." She closed her eyes for a moment before opening them again. "I just couldn't stay in the same town as him. Not then."

"He died sixteen years ago," Blake said. "Why didn't you come back?"

She sighed and sat back in her chair. "It wasn't that easy. I was still suffering some trauma from the ordeal with the horse and had to continue going through physical therapy." She smoothed her hair back from her face. "There were other changes in my life," she said, but didn't elaborate. "And maybe I was a little afraid," she added.

He frowned. "Afraid of what?"

She looked away from him for a long moment before meeting his gaze again. She touched the scar along her cheek. "Afraid of what the people I knew would think when they saw me like this."

"Like what?" He leaned forward and caught her hand on the tabletop. "What are you talking about?"

Her eyes narrowed into a confused frown. "There's no sense in dancing around it. I may have been pretty but that was a very long time ago. All of these years have passed and I'm scarred in more than one way."

Now, Blake was frowning. He clasped her hand in both of his and it felt small and warm in his grip. "You may look a little different, but you're still a beautiful woman. Who you are inside radiates out of you like it always did and that makes you one of the most gorgeous women I have ever known."

Tears glittered in her eyes. She put her free hand up to her mouth as if holding back a sob.

"You know I don't lie and I don't bullshit." He studied her and she nodded, slowly. "Take what I said and accept it as fact. Got that?"

She nodded again and moved her hand away from her mouth. "Yes," she said, her voice almost a whisper.

He took in the pain in her expression and could read everything she'd gone through over the years. It made him want to take her in his arms and protect her from anything ever happening to her again. He wanted to kiss her.

To make love to her.

Ah, hell. He dragged his hand down his face. He was in deep

shit.

Again.

As they started to leave the Hummingbird, Blake put his hand at the base of her spine, escorting her out of the restaurant. He stopped to tell Tess they'd enjoyed dinner and Cat had echoed him with compliments of her own.

On the short drive back to her house, they talked about a few of the changes in the town since she'd left.

When they reached her home, Blake parked and walked her to her front door. The soft glow of the porch light illuminated her.

She unlocked the door then paused to meet his gaze. She sounded nervous again as she said, "Would you like to come in?"

He studied her for a long moment. "I'd better not."

A look passed over her features that he couldn't identify. Disappointment? Relief? Something else?

"Thank you for a wonderful evening out." She gave a soft smile. "I had a great time."

An urge came over him that he couldn't control. Didn't want to control. He cupped her face in his hands and lowered his mouth to hers, not giving her a chance to react.

Her lips parted in surprise beneath his and he nipped at her bottom lip. She sucked in her breath and he kissed her harder. He wanted to take control of her, to possess her. He wanted her back so damned bad. The power of the feeling set him off balance.

She kissed him back. At first her kiss was tentative but then it grew in strength and matched the power of his own. Her familiar scent filled him as he inhaled and her taste brought back memories of the many kisses they had shared in the past.

Soft moans rose up from her and she gripped his shirtfront in her fists. His groin ached and he knew he was dangerously close to sweeping her up in his arms and taking her into her house and straight to bed.

He drew away, breaking the kiss. He found his breathing was hard as desire raged through him. He studied her expression and saw her eyes still wide with shock and her wet lips glistening in the porch light.

"I'm sorry." He swallowed. "I shouldn't have done that."

"Why not?" She looked puzzled at first then bit her lower lip and looked away from him.

He touched her chin and brought her back to look at him again. "You don't know how badly I want you right now. But we have too many things between us. Too much to work through."

She nodded. "We do."

He traced her lower lip with his thumb. "You'd better get inside while my willpower is intact."

She looked at him for one more long moment then drew back. "Good night, Blake." She turned and walked through her door and closed it behind her. He heard the bolt lock slide into place.

He shook his head as he looked up at the moon. "Damned fool," he muttered before heading down the stairs and back to his truck.

CHAPTER 6

The Saturday after her dinner with Blake, Cat found herself at the front door of his home clasping his files to her chest with one arm as she raised her opposite hand to knock. It hadn't taken her long to drive here and she was early.

He'd called her yesterday at work to give her directions to his ranch. Their conversation had been a little awkward and they'd talked only a few minutes before he'd had to get back to work and she needed to do so as well.

She rapped on the door and waited for someone to answer.

Thoughts of their dinner together were with her constantly. But mostly she thought about the kiss. She hadn't expected that sizzle of reaction and she had the feeling he hadn't, either.

She looked over her shoulder at the corrals and barn. He was probably out working somewhere and would be back soon.

When no one answered, she turned and moved to the edge of the porch where she sat on the top step. She tugged down her short jean skirt with one hand and held the files tight to her chest with her other as she looked over the unfamiliar ranch. When she'd known Blake before, he'd still been on his parents' ranch with his brothers.

She thought about what he'd said about his family... That they would welcome her back. Maybe she shouldn't have been so surprised. They were good people and she'd known them a long time. They had been closer family to her than her own.

The morning air felt warm and still as she let her gaze drift over the empty corrals and the quiet yard. The cattle must be out to graze and the morning chores were probably finished.

The sound of horse's hooves came from somewhere behind the house. Her heart rate picked up a bit at the prospect of seeing Blake again.

A horse and rider came around the house and Cat saw that it was Demi. Cat smiled as the blonde girl's horse trotted to the front porch and she brought the big animal to a stop.

"Hi, Demi," Cat said with a smile.

"Hi, Cat." Demi smiled in return but wore a curious expression. "What are you doing here?"

"By day, I'm an accountant." Cat held up the files. "I took over some accounts and your father's happens to be one of them. We need to go over some business."

Demi looked thoughtful and scrunched her freckled nose. "I think he's in the barn."

"What a beautiful Quarter horse." Cat set Blake's files to the side on the porch and got to her feet. She went down the stairs and to the horse and rider and then stroked the horse's forehead to her muzzle. The horse bobbed her head then snuffled at Cat's hand, checking to see if Cat had a treat. "She looks like she's a good girl," Cat said.

"She is." Demi smiled as she looked down at Cat. "Her name is Dandelion but I call her Dandy."

"I like that name." Cat continued to stroke the mare. "Do you and Dandy compete together?"

Demi nodded and leather creaked as she shifted in her saddle. "Dandy is amazing."

"From what I saw at the meeting, you're pretty amazing, too," Cat said.

"Thank you." Demi smiled again and looked over her shoulder. "I'll check and see if Dad's in the barn."

"I'll go with you," Cat said.

"All right." Demi dismounted her horse then gripped Dandy by the bridle.

"How long have you been riding?" Cat asked as she and Demi walked toward the barn, Dandy's hooves clip-clopping as they went.

"Dad let me ride with him before I could walk," Demi said. "I had a pony that I was allowed to ride when I was five. I graduated to a full-grown horse when I turned seven." She looked at Cat. "What about you?"

"I started when I joined 4-H at nine." Cat brushed a strand of hair from her face. "My family didn't have any horses but we had neighbors to the south of us who let me ride and race theirs. I used to do all of the barn chores in exchange."

They reached the barn and Cat blinked as they entered the dimness. It smelled of hay, horses, and sweet oats.

Demi started down the aisle between several stalls. "Hi, Dad." She jerked her thumb over her shoulder. "Cat's here."

Cat's belly flipped as she saw Blake come toward them. He took off a pair of work gloves and stuffed them into his back pocket before giving his daughter's braid a tweak. "Hey, kiddo."

"*Dad.*" Demi put one hand on her hip. "Don't call me that."

His gaze met Cat's and he gave her a wink, which caused her belly to flip again.

"All right, honey." He smiled at his daughter and squeezed her shoulder. "Did you arrange to go to Amy's?"

"Yeah." Demi gripped her horse's bridle. "But I'd rather be home riding."

He studied his daughter. "It's good for you to get out and be with friends and not just around your horses."

"But, I love horses." She stroked Dandy's nose. "They're more fun than people."

He smiled. "Why don't you go ahead and put Dandy up and get ready?"

"Okay." She gave an exaggerated sigh. "If you're trying to get rid of me."

With a laugh, he leaned over and kissed her on the top of her head. "Never."

Demi continued down the aisle to the back of the barn.

Cat watched Blake as he came toward her and she caught her breath at just how sexy he looked. He was dusty and sweat glistened on his skin and his jaws were a little stubbly. The sleeves of his work shirt were rolled up showing the strength in his forearms and molding his powerful biceps.

"You're early," he said as he reached her. "I'd planned to take a shower."

She swallowed. "Didn't take me as long to get here as I thought it would."

"Well, come on into the house." He indicated his home with a nod. "I'll get you a glass of iced tea and you can enjoy that while I take a quick shower."

"All right." She fell into step beside him as they started toward the ranch house.

When they reached it, she picked up his files from the porch and he held the door open as she walked inside before he closed the door behind them.

The living room was roomy with oil paintings of horses and oxblood brown leather furniture. Throw rugs were scattered on the large Mexican Saltillo tiles and a full entertainment center was along one wall.

"I love these paintings." Cat went up to one of them. Horses ran wild across an open desert in the one she was looking at. "They're beautiful."

"Demi picked them out." He turned to her as Cat raised her brows. "She loves everything to do with horses."

Impressed, Cat said, "She has great taste."

He settled his hand on her shoulder. "She likes you, so I'd have to agree."

Cat felt the strength in his touch and a vivid image rushed forward of him with his hands on her naked body. She could almost feel him caressing her breasts, teasing her nipples, and stroking her curves.

She met his gaze and heat rushed to her face. From the way he was looking at her she felt as if he could read her mind. She cleared her throat. "You mentioned iced tea?"

"I sure did." He released her shoulder and she let out her breath in a rush. "Come on into the kitchen."

With some relief, she followed him into a large kitchen with stainless steel and black appliances, cherry wood cabinets, and granite countertops.

"I love your home," she said, still carrying the files.

"We remodeled the place a year ago." Blake reached into the fridge and grabbed a clear glass pitcher of iced tea. "Put on an addition at the back of the house, including a sun porch and a guest bedroom. Demi did most of the decorating and helped pick out the cabinets and appliances. She's a natural at selecting things that look just right, like the horse paintings." The pride in his voice and on his face was clear.

"And she's only fourteen." Cat smiled as he put ice into two glasses. She set the file folders on the countertop as she added, "Although, she would have been thirteen when you remodeled a year ago."

"Yep." He nodded as he poured tea over the ice and put the pitcher back into the fridge. He handed Cat one of the glasses, then took a long drink of his own. His glass was empty when he set it down. "Make yourself at home while I take a shower."

She set her own glass down on the countertop. "Thanks."

As Blake went to his room to shower, Cat picked up the files and wandered into the living room, and admired the horse paintings again. She casually looked around the living room and at the family photographs on the mantel. Demi was in most of them by herself—a few showing her astride her horse and holding trophies and rosettes. Blake was with her in a couple of the other photographs wearing a smile of fatherly pride.

The front door opened and Cat glanced in that direction. Demi walked in and shut the door behind her.

"You have great taste." Cat gestured toward the paintings.

Demi's face lit up. "I love horses."

"I was like you when I was growing up." Cat slipped her free hand into a pocket in her short jean skirt. "I lived and breathed horses."

"That does sound exactly like me." Demi took off her western hat. Her blonde hair was in a smooth braid that fell down her back. "I need to get ready to go to Amy's."

"Be sure and tell her hello for me," Cat said.

"I will." Demi headed down a hallway, disappearing from sight.

Moments later, Blake returned. The dust and sweat was gone and his short hair was damp. A white T-shirt pulled tight across his muscular chest and he wasn't wearing a belt. He hadn't shaved and still had stubble on his jaws.

"Let's go to my office." He gave a nod indicating that she should follow him.

With one hand, she smoothed down her blouse and jean skirt as she followed him, her throat suddenly dry.

When he reached the doorway to his office, he gestured for her to go in before him. As she passed him she caught his clean scent of soap and shampoo.

Inside the office was a large oak desk with a leather chair behind it as well as two chairs in front of the desk. There were wood file cabinets along one wall. She walked up to the wall of bookshelves and saw that books by Harold Bell Wright, Zane Grey, and Max Brand filled them as well as classics by Mark Twain, Charles Dickens, and D.H. Lawrence, and more, much more.

He also had books on things like anatomy and physiology, and books related to agricultural subjects. Horse and cattlemen magazines were scattered on a credenza.

When they were young, Blake had always loved to read before he went to bed. He had a thirst for knowledge that she'd never seen in anyone else.

She turned to face him. "Did you go to Northern Arizona University like you always planned?"

He shook his head. "Arizona State for four years."

"So we're rivals." She laughed and he grinned. "U of A and ASU have been bitter opponents for over a century. What made you decide to go to ASU?"

"ASU has a better business degree program." He moved behind the big oak desk. "Where do you want to start?"

She sat in one of the chairs in front of his desk and crossed her legs at the knees. She opened the file on her lap. "I have the copy of the notice from the IRS here. I guess we'd better start with the first year you're being audited."

About half an hour later, Demi walked into the office. She had a duffel bag slung over one shoulder and was holding a present wrapped in light purple with a big dark purple bow. "Dad, Amy's mom is here to pick me up. She said she'll drop me off tomorrow afternoon."

Blake got up from behind his desk and went to his daughter. He gave her a kiss on the forehead. "Have a good time, honey."

She kissed his cheek. "I'll try," she said, but smiled. She looked at Cat and gave her a little wave. "Bye, Cat."

"Have fun." Cat returned the wave.

Demi ducked out of the office and a few moments later Cat heard the opening and closing of the front door.

Cat was suddenly aware of the fact that she and Blake were all alone now. A tension seemed to develop in the air between them and their gazes met and held for a long moment.

She looked away, her eyes going to the papers spread out on the desk in front of her. "I guess we'd better get back to work."

When she met his gaze again, he gave a slow nod. "I guess we'd better."

CHAPTER 7

"I guess that will have to do for today." Cat brushed her hair out of her eyes as she started to organize the papers on Blake's desk. "We can work on this more another day." She glanced from the papers to him. He was sitting in the chair beside her now, in front of the desk. "My schedule is still pretty open," she said. "When is a good time for us to get together again?"

He was studying her, his gaze so intense that she felt the heat of it on her skin. "Friday night at seven," he said.

"Friday night?" It took a moment to register that he was asking her out. "Oh." She hesitated and he kept looking at her with that same dark look. "I—sure."

She felt warning bells going off in her head, but too late. It wasn't good to spend so much time with the man. She was going to fall head over heels for him again.

If she hadn't already.

She looked away from the intensity of his gaze and got to her feet. From her peripheral vision she saw him stand, then felt the heat of his body when he moved closer to her.

"I think we made pretty good progress." Her heart pounded faster and she busied herself with making each stack on the desktop perfectly neat. "We might be able to get everything done in one more meeting." She rushed her words, feeling like she was babbling.

"KitCat." His voice was soft and she went still at the low, throbbing quality of it.

Slowly, she lifted her eyes to meet his. He was looking at her intently. Her lips parted, but she couldn't think of a thing to say.

He took her by the shoulders, bringing her face to face with him. "Damn, Cat. I don't know how much longer I can be around you without having you."

Her eyes widened and her lips parted. He wanted her?

He gripped her upper arms tighter, the pressure of his fingers almost hurting her. "Damn," he said again before he jerked her up against him and brought his mouth hard down on hers.

She gasped as he took control of her mouth, kissing her hard. It was more primal than the night before, almost wild. She didn't remember him kissing like this before. It was as if the man he had been before had matured, becoming more dominant and decisive. She knew he'd decided he was going to have her. If she said no, he'd let her go, but she didn't want to say no. She wanted him.

A groan rose up in him and she followed his lead, letting him take the kiss to a level of passion she'd never experienced before.

He released her shoulders and slid his hands over her blouse to her waist then cupped her ass and pulled her up tight to him. The feel of his erection against her belly sent fire through her straight between her thighs.

She breathed in his clean, masculine scent and reveled in his taste and the feel of his hands on her. She moved her hands up his chest, feeling the soft cotton of his T-shirt beneath her palms, and then she wrapped her arms around his neck and pressed her breasts against him.

When he broke the kiss, he moved his lips along her jawline to her throat. His stubble felt rough against her skin but something about the sandpapery feel of it made her even more excited.

"I'm not going to be able to help myself with you." He groaned as he pulled her short skirt above her ass and felt the silky panties underneath. The heat of his palms burned through the thin material to her skin and it almost felt like she was wearing nothing at all. "Hell, you'd better tell me now if you want to stop."

"Don't stop." She moaned, as he trailed his lips and tongue from the hollow of her throat to the V in her blouse.

He whirled her so that she was backed up against the desk and she had to brace her hands on the stacks of papers to either side of her in order to balance herself. She arched her back as he moved his hands to the buttons on her blouse. His big fingers fumbled with the buttons and he gave a low growl and grasped the material.

Buttons flew and she gasped as he tore the blouse open. She heard the ping of buttons but was barely conscious of them as he pushed her blouse over her shoulders and down her arms before she shook it the rest of the way off. Tearing her blouse off was something he'd never done before and the wildness of it made her squirm with desire.

He unfastened the front clasp of her bra, releasing her breasts, and she helped him take the bra the rest of the way off.

"I've never forgotten how beautiful your breasts are." He cupped them as he met her gaze. "I've dreamed of them." He lowered his head and sucked one of her nipples hard enough to bring tears to her eyes. Tears of pleasure and pain.

"I've dreamed of you, too," she whispered.

He grasped her ass, lifted her, and set her on the papers and files spread out on the desk's surface. She continued to brace herself with her palms on the papers as he moved between her legs, the rough material of his jeans rubbing against the insides of her thighs. He tugged off his T-shirt and tossed it aside. He was so big and powerful, the veins standing out on his biceps, as he seemed to fight for control.

He put his hands on the desk to either side of her thighs and stared intently into her eyes. "I'm going to fuck you, KitCat. I'm going to see what it feels like being inside you again."

Moisture dampened her between her thighs at the rough, erotic way he was talking to her. It sent thrills through her and she nodded. "Yes."

He grasped the sides of her black panties and tugged them down. She raised her hips a little and he jerked the material all the way off. Then, he unbuttoned her skirt and pulled it off as well. She was naked, wide open, and exposed now, ready for him. She expected him to unbutton his jeans, which had a thick bulge behind the tough cotton and then drive into her.

But he lowered himself so that he was kneeling between her thighs. He slid his palms beneath her ass and buried his face against her folds.

Her eyes went wide and she cried out as he licked and sucked her clit. He slid a finger into her core and moved it in and out as he went down on her.

Colors and sensations swirled in her mind as she watched him, his head between her thighs and his eyes meeting hers. He flicked his tongue over the hard nub and she could barely keep her eyes open so that she could watch him.

Her climax came closer and closer and she knew she wasn't going to be able to hold back. It rose inside her and her thighs started to tremble.

The orgasm burst inside her and she jerked and cried out as her body throbbed and shook from the power of her climax.

He was kicking off his boots and unfastening his jeans as she came down from the pinnacle she'd just climbed. She watched him, dazed, as his big, thick cock was released from his clothing and then he was as naked as she was.

He grasped her by the waist, flipped her over so that her belly and breasts were on the desk with papers and files beneath her, and then his cock was pressed against her ass. "You know how I like it from behind."

"Yes." The word hissed from her.

She heard the sound of foil tearing and knew he must have had a condom in his wallet. A moment later he spread her open then placed the head of his cock against her core. He grasped her hips and slammed himself inside her.

She nearly screamed from the exquisite pleasure and pain of the suddenness of him stretching her and filling her. It had been so long since she'd had sex, and no one could ever have compared to Blake.

"Damn, you're tight." He began taking her, hard and fast.

Papers that had been stacked so neatly began flying off the desk, folders sliding off and thumping onto the floor.

He took her like a wild man, growling deep in his throat. Just when she was about to climax again, he pulled out, causing her to whimper.

And then he was flipping her onto her back, more papers flying onto the floor. Her back was slick with sweat and she could feel papers sticking to her skin.

"I want to see your eyes as you watch me take you." He hooked her thighs around his and drove into her again.

It was so difficult to keep her eyes open as she was carried away by the sensations. He grasped her breasts and pinched her nipples as he drove in and out, pinching them so hard it made her eyes widen in surprise.

Sweat rolled down the side of his face and his expression was almost pained, his eyes dark with passion. His jaw tensed and she knew he was close to coming. She recognized that look from all those years ago.

Her second orgasm came out of nowhere. She cried out and then he was shouting as he came inside her. She felt the throb of his cock in time with the pulsing in her core.

And then he was bracing his hands to either side of her, looking down at her as his groin pressed tight against hers, his cock still inside her.

He gave her a gentle kiss then smiled at her. "It's damned good to have you back, KitCat, and although it was great, I'm not talking about the sex."

She smiled up at him. "That was some welcome home."

"Just wait 'til we have seconds," he said and kissed her again.

CHAPTER 8

Cat shifted on Blake's bed, snuggling closer to him, his bare skin warm against hers. He held her with one arm while he lay on his back, her head resting on his shoulder. He slowly stroked her arm with his fingertips. His scent filled her and she felt content for the first time in a long time.

She smiled, loving the moment yet knowing it couldn't last forever. Her stomach growled and he gave a soft chuckle.

"Let's get something to eat." He ran his finger along her nose to the tip. "All this great sex has helped work up an appetite. And then I have my evening chores to take care of."

She nodded and her hair slid like silk across his chest. "Sounds good to me."

They both slid out of bed. He gave her one of his T-shirts

to wear, clearly remembering that she'd always loved to wear his T-shirts when they'd dated. She slipped into it and realized it fit her even looser than his shirts had when he was a young man.

"You look so damned cute." He kissed her then slid on a pair of boxer briefs and a nice snug pair of Wrangler jeans.

"And you look so damned hot," she said, admiring his bare chest and the way the jeans hung low on his hips.

He put his arm around her shoulders and she slipped her hand around his waist as they walked to the kitchen. Through the huge windows she could see the sun was lowering, the western horizon deepening to yellows, oranges, and dark blue.

She glanced at the clock. "It's nearly seven-thirty. No wonder I'm hungry."

"What would you like for dinner?" He released her and went to the fridge. "For something quick, there's a pan of leftover enchiladas along with guacamole, salsa, and chips."

"Perfect." She pushed her hair out of her face. "What do you want me to do?"

He grabbed the salsa and guacamole and handed them to her then took out the enchiladas. While heating the pan of them in the microwave, they set the table and got out a bag of chips along with the pitcher of iced tea and a couple of glasses. When the enchiladas were finished heating, they sat and he served generous helpings with a spatula.

She dug in and made a satisfied sound. "Fantastic." She looked at him to see he was looking at her with an amused expression. "What?"

"It's good to have you here, KitCat." A smile curved his mouth.

She gave him a smile in return. "It's good to be here." She cut into another piece of enchilada.

"How's your grandmother?" he asked.

"Not so good." Cat felt concern ball in her chest. "That's why I came back."

He studied her. "Is there anything I can do?"

"I don't think so." Cat shook her head. "But I think she's glad to have me back."

"I am, too," he said, his voice low and serious.

She sought to change the subject. "Your daughter is a special girl."

He smiled. "She is."

"So, you have full custody?" Cat asked.

"Since she was six." His expression didn't change, but Cat sensed tension in him. She wasn't going to ask anything more, but he volunteered the information, his look becoming serious. "Sally, her mother, ran off with a man she met in rehab to God knows where. I filed for divorce and full custody and she didn't contest it."

"It's hard to believe a mother could abandon her child like that," Cat said quietly.

"I sure as hell couldn't believe it." He shook his head. "We married because she got pregnant and I wanted to do the right thing. It wasn't easy, but at least Demi had both her parents." His expression darkened. "Then Sally changed. It was like something inside her just snapped and she didn't want to be a mother anymore, much less stay married to a man she didn't love."

Cat looked down at her plate, her thoughts turning over what he'd said. She looked at Blake again. "I can't imagine what you and Demi must have gone through."

"The worst part was explaining to Demi that her mother had

left and I didn't know if she was coming back." His jaw tightened. "She did return a couple of years ago and I agreed to try to make it work so that Demi could have her mother. It didn't last long and she was gone again."

Blake had never been much of a talker, and Cat was surprised that he was sharing as much as he was.

"Sally has been moved from place to place with no stability," Blake continued, and his eyes narrowed. "But not too long ago she contacted Demi and told her she has an apartment in Prescott and she wants Demi to stay with her."

"Are you going to let her?" Cat asked.

He rubbed his hand over his head. "I sure as hell don't want to. But damned if I know what's the right thing to do."

She nodded. "That's a tough situation to be in."

"Yeah, it is." He shook his head. "Demi needs a woman's influence in her life, but as far as I'm concerned, her mother isn't the right influence. But I don't know if I'm enough."

Cat reached across the table and put her hand on his. "I'd say you've done an incredible job of raising your daughter. I'm sure you're doing more than enough."

He turned his hand over and held hers. "Did you have any serious relationships after Toby Jennings?"

She was suddenly aware of the scar again and it tingled. She had forgotten it the entire time she'd been with Blake. With him it didn't seem to matter at all.

"One." She took a deep breath and drew her hand away from his. "I married a man…"

"I didn't realize you'd been married," Blake said.

"Yes." She bit her lower lip as familiar pain ripped through her. She met his gaze. "We had a daughter. We lost her when she was four."

Blake's face registered shock. "Oh, honey. Damn, I'm sorry."

Cat wiped away a tear. It didn't matter how many years had passed, her heart broke all over again whenever she talked about Melanie. "She would have been close to Demi's age now."

He took both of her hands and squeezed them. "I can't imagine what you've gone through. Damn." He shook his head. "If anything happened to Demi…"

Cat squeezed his hands in return. "Melanie was a blessing in my life. I thank God for the time we had together. She's with me wherever I go. She's my angel."

He gave a slow nod, his expression showing so much compassion that it made her heart squeeze.

She took a deep breath and went back to what they'd been talking about. "I've dated but there's never been a man I've truly fallen in love with. Not since—" She was going to say "not since you," but she didn't complete the thought.

He studied her and filled it in with, "Not since Toby or your ex."

"To be honest, Toby and I were never that serious. He'd been an escape. A way out of Prescott. I thought that maybe we had something real, but I realized after he left that it wasn't." She waved her hand like waving Toby away. "As far as my ex, I would consider him a total mistake if it hadn't been for my daughter."

Blake looked thoughtful but didn't ask her any more questions.

They had finished eating before she realized it. "I guess I should head home," she said as they cleaned the dishes and put everything away.

"Why don't you spend the night?" He grasped her by the shoulders and searched her gaze. "Demi said Amy's mother will drop her off sometime in the afternoon."

Cat bit her lower lip. Was it a good idea? The more time she spent around Blake, the more likely she was going to fall for him again.

But she didn't want to leave. She wanted to feel his arms around her and wake up in the morning with his body next to hers.

He lightly stroked the curve of her face. "Say yes, KitCat."

It felt so good to hear him call her that again. She couldn't help herself and said, "Okay."

He smiled. "I've got to take care of those chores first."

She smiled. "I'll help."

When they were finished, they headed back into the house. She'd enjoyed helping him feed the animals and take care of other chores around the ranch.

"How about a movie?" he asked once they were inside.

"Sure." She tilted her head to the side. "What do you have?"

"Let's go take a look."

They agreed on a movie that had recently come out on DVD. He set it up and they cuddled on one end of the couch. He had his arm around her and she rested her head on his shoulder, her bare legs curled under her on the couch.

It felt good being with him again, and so natural that it surprised her. It was like they started right back where they'd left off, only they were a lot older now. So much had happened over the past nearly two decades, in each of their lives, and it had changed them, shaped them.

Yet here they were.

The movie wasn't half over when he adjusted her in his arms and kissed her. His kiss made her forget everything but being with him. It was slow and sensual and made her head feel like it was spinning.

Something about his kiss was magic, transporting her to another place and time. She slipped her hand up his bare chest to his neck and slid her hand into the short strands of his hair. She liked the way it felt against her fingers.

He brought her onto his lap, still kissing her, a groan rumbling up inside him and she answered it with a soft moan. She wanted him again, was ready for him in so many ways. He moved his hand to her breast and it felt so warm through the cotton of the T-shirt she was wearing. His T-shirt. The material had been rubbing her nipples all night and his touch made her nipples feel even more sensitive.

"I think I need some rope," he murmured. "I'll tie you to my bed and won't let you get away."

"Promise?" she whispered.

Still holding her in his arms, he stood in a motion so quick it caught her off guard and she cried out and held onto his neck. His gaze held hers for a long moment before he carried her back to his bedroom.

CHAPTER 9

Early the following morning, the front door opened then slammed shut. "Dad, I'm home."

Blake almost groaned. Damn. Demi wasn't supposed to be home until the afternoon. He'd had made a point of never having women over when his daughter was home.

He paused before bringing the gallon of milk out of the fridge, then closed the door and walked to the counter where two tall glasses waited for Cat and himself.

Cat had been just about to take a bite out of a cinnamon roll and had gone still, hand and roll frozen in midair. She was sitting at the kitchen table and was wearing one of his T-shirts with panties beneath that but no bra.

He met Cat's gaze and tried to give her a reassuring look. She didn't look the least bit reassured.

"In the kitchen, honey," he called out to Demi. He started pouring milk into one of the glasses as his daughter walked into the kitchen. "Do you want a cinnamon roll and milk?"

Demi walked into the kitchen and her gaze stopped on Cat. She spun to face her father. "I saw Cat's truck and thought she came over early. But she spent the night, didn't she," Demi stated in a furious tone. "She's even wearing your T-shirt."

Cat had blushed even before Demi had entered the kitchen. She set down her cinnamon roll on her plate. She wiped her fingers on a napkin and tugged down the T-shirt.

"Right now she's having breakfast with me." He carried the two glasses of milk to the table and set one in front of Cat. "Do you want some?"

A flush crept over his daughter's face as she gripped her duffel bag tighter. "So, she really did spend the night?"

There was no sense in lying about it. His daughter was a smart girl, and he wouldn't insult her intelligence.

"Yes." He pulled up his chair at the table, across from Cat, but didn't sit down. "How was your time at Amy's?"

"I can't believe you slept with her." Demi's knuckles were turning white as she gripped the strap of her duffel.

"Demi." He kept his voice calm. "You can either join us for breakfast or you can take your things to your room."

"That's why you wanted me to go to Amy's. You didn't want me here." She glared at him and Cat before she whirled and ran down the hall.

Cat's eyes were wide as she turned to look at him. "I should have gone home last night."

He shook his head. "It's not your fault. I thought Demi wouldn't be back until late this afternoon."

"I feel awful." Cat scooted back her chair. "I should go."

He leaned over the table and touched her wrist. "Stay. It's too late and you might as well eat your breakfast."

She nodded and brought her chair back up to the table, but she didn't look happy as she tore off a piece of the cinnamon roll and stared at it before setting it down again.

"I'm not going to let a good thing like what we've had be ruined." He held her gaze. "Okay?"

She didn't look convinced, but she nodded again.

"I need to go and talk with Demi." He pushed his chair back up to the table. "I'll be back."

"Yes," Cat said.

He rubbed his scalp with his hand as he headed down the hall to Demi's room. Damn. This wasn't the way he'd wanted his daughter to know he was in a relationship with a woman.

Was that what it was? A relationship?

Yeah, it was, as far as he was concerned. He wasn't into one-night stands and he'd never think of Cat that way.

This time Demi's door wasn't closed all of the way. He knocked and paused before he pushed the door all the way open.

She was lying on her bed facedown, a pillow over her head so that he couldn't see her face.

He sat on the edge of her bed, close to her. "Hey, kiddo."

"Don't call me that," came her muffled voice from beneath the pillow.

He gently pulled the pillow off her head and set it aside, against her stuffed horse. Her cheek rested on the mattress, facing him, but she wouldn't meet his eyes.

"We need to talk about this." He reached out and smoothed strands of blonde hair from her cheek.

"That's why you wanted me to go to Amy's so bad." A sob came out of her throat. "You didn't want me around."

"That's not true." He continued to stroke her hair. "What happened with Cat and me…I never expected it. The fact that she spent the night had nothing to do with me encouraging you to go to Amy's."

She was silent a long moment.

"Honey, are you all right?" he asked.

"No." Tears glistened on her lashes as she met his gaze. Whenever she cried a part of him ached inside. "How can you and Mom get back together if you're dating other women?"

He was taken aback for a moment before he said, "Your mom and I aren't going to get back together. We tried it, honey, and it didn't work."

"You didn't try hard enough." Demi turned onto her side, facing him, and hugged her pillow to her. "I want my mom."

His heart squeezed. What could he say that would make her feel better? If only Sally was stable they could share custody and she could be with her mother at least part of the time. But that wasn't going to happen because Sally had proven time and again that she wasn't a good influence on Demi or a fit mother. She'd had problems with drugs and alcohol. Not to mention, man after man coming through her life and her moving from place to place, never settling down for long.

He hadn't wanted Demi to witness other women in his own life, especially because she saw that happening with her mother time and again, one man after another. It was unfortunate that she'd come home when she had. Eventually, he would have let her know that he and Cat were in a relationship, but not like this.

"You barely know Cat." Demi sniffled. "At least not anymore."

With a sigh, he rested his hand on her arm. "I loved Cat deeply, and for a very long time. Love like that never really goes away."

Demi studied him with her red-rimmed eyes. "Did you ever love Mom?"

For a moment, he debated on what to tell her. Again, he settled for the truth. "No, honey. We never really knew each other that well. We married because your mother got pregnant."

"With me," Demi said flatly. "So if I had never been born, you would never have married her."

"You were and are a blessing to me." He gently squeezed her arm. "You're the best thing that has ever happened in my life. I have no regrets and I thank God that she did get pregnant with you. I wish things could have been different with your mother, but they weren't. What counts is that I have you." He emphasized the last three words.

"What about Cat?" Demi looked away from him. "How do you feel about her?"

"I—" He paused. "All I know is that I care about her and I want to see what happens with us."

"That doesn't mean I have to like it." Demi scowled as she turned back to him again. "I don't like it at all."

"No, you don't have to." He lightly rubbed her back. "But I hope you'll give Cat a chance."

Demi said nothing, just looked stubbornly away.

He leaned down and kissed her cheek. "I love you, honey."

Her eyes met his. "I love you, too, Daddy." She rarely called him Daddy, and it made him want to smile.

He got to his feet and looked down at her. "Do you want some breakfast?"

"I ate at Amy's." She scooted up in the bed but looked away from him "I came home early because I want to practice for the upcoming rodeo."

He gave a nod. "I'll time you."

"No." She glanced toward the door. "I don't want *her* there."

"Cat was planning on leaving soon." He looked at his daughter steadily. "But even if she wasn't, I expect you to treat her with respect. Do you understand?"

Demi scowled and didn't answer.

"Demi," he said with a note of warning in his tone, "do you understand?"

She crossed her arms over her chest. "Yeah. I understand."

"Good." He smoothed her hair that was pulled back in its customary braid. "Why don't you get ready for practice and I'll be out there as soon as I'm able to?"

She looked away again. "I'll don't feel like it anymore."

"Don't let being upset tarnish or interrupt what you love to do," he said before turning and walking to the door of his daughter's room. He paused and looked over his shoulder to see her still looking away with her arms crossed. He closed the door behind him.

He returned to the kitchen and saw that the cinnamon rolls were covered under the domed serving tray and the milk put away. Dishes were drying in the dish rack.

Cat wasn't there. He went to the front window and looked out. Her truck was gone.

He dragged his hand down his face, wondering if he should go after her now. But no, Cat was a grown woman and they'd work through this later. Right now he needed to spend some time with his daughter.

CHAPTER 10

Cat wanted to bang her head against the steering wheel as she drove back to town from Blake's ranch. The last thing she wanted was to get between him and his daughter. She should have gone home last night just to be safe.

Next Saturday was another meeting with the 4-H horse club and Demi would be there. Right now Cat wasn't sure how she felt…embarrassed? Or did she just feel bad at being there when the girl had come home? She wondered how she would feel when she saw Blake's daughter again, and how Demi would feel about her.

When Cat reached her small house, she parked her truck in the driveway, killed the engine, and climbed out. She jogged up the porch stairs as she dug her keys out of her purse, then opened the front door and closed it behind her before tossing her purse onto the couch and heading to her bedroom.

She left a trail of clothing on her bedroom floor as she made her way to her bathroom. A shower was what she needed now. When the water was heated, she stepped beneath the spray and found herself thinking about yesterday afternoon and night with Blake. She warmed at the memory of his hands on her, his body on hers, the feel of him inside her. Wild tingling went through her at the thoughts.

It had been even more incredible than she remembered it being when they were young. He was more experienced and his body was different—more muscular, more powerful. She'd loved the feel of being in his arms and cuddling up to him.

She washed her face under the spray and stopped as her fingers brushed the scar. The moment her fingertips touched the thick smooth skin, all of her insecurities came rushing back. Blake hadn't seemed to care how different she looked or about the mar across her features. It was like he saw *her*, who she was inside.

But how could he not notice? How could he not care about her scars?

A twisting sensation in her midsection made her hold one arm to her abdomen. She looked down at her belly and remembered when she'd been pregnant. She'd always wanted children and when Melanie had been born, everything in her life had seemed to have new purpose. When her daughter had died... All of that had changed.

She still wanted children. Not to replace Melanie, but because she had so much love to give and children were so precious. She imagined what it would be like to have Blake's child. The thought came out of nowhere.

After she toweled off, she dressed in a worn pair of jeans and faded red University of Arizona T-shirt. As she tugged on socks and her athletic shoes, she thought about what she had planned for the day. On Sundays she always spent time at her grandmother's home and helped her with anything she needed to have taken care of.

Of course Grandmother Hayden intended to make fried chicken and would be serving it with all of the traditional sides despite the fact it would be just the two of them. Cat would end up with enough leftovers to last her for days.

Before she left, she did the laundry, ran the dishwasher, and took care of a few other things she needed to do to get ready for the week ahead.

When she was finished, she picked up her cell phone and saw that she had missed a call and had a message. The number was familiar but it took a moment to realize it was Blake's. She hadn't saved his number in her contacts yet. Her stomach flipped as she listened to the short message.

"Hi, Cat." Blake's voice was deep and sexy. "Call me."

She considered returning his call but decided not to, at least not right now. Just the thought of him brought back thoughts of the time they'd spent together. It had seemed natural...and it had been good. *Really* good.

If that wasn't an understatement, she didn't know what was.

"Time to go to Grandma's," she said to Sam as the hamster scampered around his habitat. "See you when I get back."

Sam paused and stood on his hind legs before ducking into a tube and wriggling through it. Cat laughed and shook her head. Yes, hamsters were so much simpler than men.

When Cat arrived at Grandma Hayden's, she waved to the neighbor who was planting flowers in the beds near the house in the front yard. To the right of Grandma's door was a pair of red metal rocking chairs with white arm rests and to the left was a porch swing for two.

After she let herself into the house, Cat tossed her purse on the couch and headed out back to find her grandmother hanging up her wash on a clothesline in the backyard.

She didn't bother telling her grandmother that she should get a clothes dryer. The older woman would just argue that she didn't believe the expense was warranted when she didn't have that many clothes to dry and she was perfectly capable of hanging them up herself.

Cat stepped through the back screen door and walked down the creaking wooden steps to the back yard and joined her grandmother beneath the clothesline.

"How are you this morning, Grandma?" Cat asked as she picked up a white housedress with sprigs of flowers on it and used two wooden clothespins to secure it to the line.

"It's a beautiful day and I'm still alive and kicking." Grandma Hayden gave Cat a smile. "I'd say I'm doing pretty well."

Cat smiled back as she pinned up a blue washcloth. A breeze caused the clothing and linens to flap in the sunshine. Together, Cat and her grandmother put a set of flowered sheets on one of the lines and they billowed in the light wind. Cat loved the smell of clean linens and the cool feel of the damp cloth against her hands as she hung them up.

Grandma hung up a slip. "You spend far too much time with an old woman."

"I love time with you." Cat smiled. "Why do you think I came back permanently?"

Grandma Hayden looked at Cat. "You didn't have to come out here just for me, but it's darned good to have you here."

"It's good to be here." Cat gave her grandmother a kiss on her soft, papery cheek.

When they finished hanging up the laundry, Grandma Hayden said, "I'm going to start supper now."

"Can't wait." Cat carried the laundry basket on her hip as she followed her grandmother up the back steps into the house. "What can I do?"

Grandma Hayden glanced over her shoulder. "Why don't you help me make the biscuits?"

"Sure." Cat nodded.

Cat's grandmother paused on the top step and held her hand to her stomach. Pain flashed across her face.

"Grandma?" Cat's heart squeezed. "Are you okay?"

The pain vanished from Grandma Hayden's face. She gave Cat a smile that looked a little forced. "I'm fine." She turned and pulled open the screen door.

The screen door squeaked as they walked through it and it made a thumping sound when Cat let it go behind her. The sight of her grandmother in pain made her ache inside. She latched the screen door with its hook then set the plastic laundry basket on top of the washing machine before going into the kitchen.

Her grandmother had just finished tying on a flowered apron with frills on the hem. Likely she'd made it herself.

"How's that boy doing?" Grandma Hayden asked as she brought a package of chicken out from the fridge.

"Boy?" Cat's brows knitted together. Then it dawned on her. She meant Blake. All of Cat's friends from when she was young were still "boy" or "girl" to Grandma Hayden.

Cat's body heated like it always did when she thought about Blake, the man. How did Grandma Hayden know if she'd even seen Blake since she'd been back?

"Blake McBride," Grandma said. "Who else would I be talking about, girl?"

Cat swallowed as she took baking powder out of the pantry. "He's doing good. Did you know he has a daughter?"

"I've run into him a time or two over the past nearly twenty years," the older woman said. "The last time I saw him…must have been a couple of years ago now. His little girl was with him. Cute little blonde thing."

"She is cute." Cat nodded, trying not to think about this morning and the dismayed look on Demi's face.

"And?" Grandma Hayden gave her a sly look as she got out flour for the biscuits and to coat the chicken.

"His daughter is in the 4-H horse club that I'm leading now." Cat got measuring cups and spoons out. "Not to mention, he's a client at my accounting firm."

"And you went out with him to the Hummingbird this week," Grandma Hayden said.

"I was going to tell you, but I didn't get a chance." Cat cut her gaze to her grandmother. "How did you know?"

"I have my ways." The older woman gave a mysterious smile. "How was it, dear?"

"It was nice." Cat smiled as she thought about the fondue and the kiss.

"He's a good boy." Grandma Hayden nodded. "You couldn't do any better."

Cat shook her head. "Just because I'm back doesn't mean that Blake and I are going to get back together, Grandma."

With a shrug, her grandmother said, "You two belong together. You always have."

"Things have changed," Cat said quietly. "We're different people now."

Grandma Hayden set aside the paprika she'd been shaking into the coating she was making for the chicken. She spoke in her no-nonsense voice as she eyed Cat. "Don't let anything like a little scar change how you feel about yourself, Catharine Hayden. Don't let it hold you back. You're a beautiful young woman and you'd better start believing that."

Her grandmother had always seemed to know what was bothering her no matter how much she tried to hide it.

Cat didn't look at her grandmother for a long moment. When she did, she went for a smile. "I love you, Grandma."

"Don't try to change the subject," her grandmother said, but smiled.

"I'm afraid." Cat bit her lower lip before she continued. "If I fall for him again and he doesn't feel the same way about me... I don't know if my heart can take that."

"You can't live your life afraid, Catharine." Grandma Hayden adjusted her apron. "You go after what will make you happy. If things don't work out you move on. What are those lines from that poem? 'Tis better to have loved and lost...'"

"Than never to have loved at all," Cat finished.

"I always did like Tennyson." Grandma Hayden went back to

preparing the chicken. "You remember that, girl."

Cat thought about what her grandmother had said. "I will, Grandma."

At least she'd try.

CHAPTER 11

Cat sat astride the horse that had almost killed her. It was Firestorm. Fear shot through her belly but she tried not to let the horse know she was afraid. If he knew she was afraid he would try to throw her and try to kill her again.

She and Firestorm were alone in the middle of a rodeo arena, the sun shining, the wind blowing just enough to raise her hair above her shoulders and causing small dust devils to swirl in the dirt around Firestorm's hooves.

A presence caused her to look to her right and she saw Blake astride a mare beside her and Firestorm. Blake's presence was solid and comforting, yet he was staring ahead and his features appeared tight, as if he was in some kind of pain.

She turned to see what he was looking at and she froze. People she knew stood in an arc in front of them now, coming out of nowhere. And they were laughing and pointing. At her.

Heated embarrassment burned her skin. Her friend, Jackie... Penny, the waitress... The Hummingbird's hostess, Tess... Marsha Solara, the accountant she worked with... The kids from the 4-H horse club... Eddie, her ex-husband... Toby... Demi.

All pointing and laughing at her.

"Look at her. Look at that scar. Isn't she ugly?"

Tears backed up behind Cat's eyes. She looked at Blake and saw something like pain on his face as he looked at her tormentors. He said nothing.

She clenched her fists on Firestorm's reins and prepared to take off, but something kept her and the horse frozen to the spot, unable to escape the ridicule.

"Please stop," she sobbed the words.

Tears flowing down her cheeks, she whirled Firestorm around and they bolted toward barrels she hadn't noticed before. She ignored Blake's call to her and the horse galloped faster.

The fear she felt at being astride the horse that had almost killed her, magnified. What was she doing riding him?

But pain filled her heart so much that she almost didn't care.

Firestorm reached the barrels and they started racing the familiar cloverleaf pattern. She urged the horse to move faster and faster and he followed her commands.

But, when they reached the last barrel, Firestorm came to a complete stop, almost throwing her. Terror caused her to scream and she clung to the saddle horn as the gelding reared up on his hind legs and she almost fell.

She fought for control but there was no controlling the horse.

She screamed again then found herself airborne.

The doctor's words rang in her ears as she sailed through the air in an impossibly long arc. "You shouldn't ride horses anymore… Next time you might not be so lucky."

Vaguely she saw Blake running toward her, fear on his strong features. His shout was faint to her ears.

The ground came up to meet her in a rush.

She screamed again.

"No." Cat thrashed. "No."

She opened her eyes and realized she was in her own bed as her ceiling came into focus. Tangled around her legs, her sheets were damp from perspiration.

"Damn." She rubbed her eyes and found they were wet.

Her heart continued to pound as if she was really in that arena and had just been thrown. The terror had been so real that she almost couldn't separate her emotions.

She realized she was clenching her hands in her sleep shirt at her chest. She tried to relax her grip but couldn't unclench her fingers.

It had been so long since she'd had a nightmare about riding Firestorm. This was the first time other people had been present.

Taking deep breaths, she tried to calm down and slow her heart rate. It wasn't real. It wasn't real. It was just a nightmare.

Her head started to ache and she was afraid a migraine was coming on. She always ended up with a migraine after dreaming about Firestorm.

She had to get a grip. It was Monday morning and she needed to get to work. She sat up, untangled herself from the sheets, scooted out of bed, and headed to the bathroom. The ugliness of the nightmare clung to her skin like pond scum and she needed to take a shower to scrub it off.

When she walked into the bathroom she paused and looked at her reflection in the mirror. The scar seemed so much more vivid than ever. She moved closer to the mirror and traced the slash across her face. Her eyes were a little red from the tears the dream had brought forth—not only because of the horse, but because of the people being so cruel.

She shook her head. She hadn't cried over the scar in a long time.

Blake had been there, too. He'd been standing beside her, but he'd looked upset. Had the dream-Blake been thinking the same thing everyone else had been saying?

With a shake of her head she turned away and ran the water in the shower until it was warm. No, Blake would never think of her that way.

Yet doubt and insecurities kept dragging her down.

She opened the medicine cabinet and took out the bottle of migraine meds that would hopefully help stave off a full-blown migraine. She shook out a couple of tablets, cupped water from the sink in her hand, then swallowed the meds and washed them down with the water in her palm.

When she stepped under the showerhead, she let the spray hit her full-force in the face. The awful feelings the dream had caused in her seemed to fade as the water washed over her and her mind cleared. She shook off the insecurities and fear that the nightmare had dredged up.

When she reached the accounting firm, Blake had his shoulder hitched up against a column of the overhang in front of the door. Her heart thumped a little faster when she saw him.

Thoughts of the nightmare came rushing at her and she remembered how he'd been at her side and how upset he'd looked.

She forced thoughts of the dream away, parked her truck next to his, and climbed out. She shut and locked the door, then walked up to meet him.

"You didn't return my two calls yesterday," he said in a slow drawl as he pushed away from the column and met her in front of the office. "Is everything all right?"

"I went to my grandmother's and stayed a little late." Cat gave him an apologetic smile. "I had Sunday supper with her and then we played dominoes and watched an old movie. She really seemed to need company last night."

Blake put his hand on her shoulder and leaned down and kissed her, catching her off guard. "I missed you," he said in a low voice as he drew away. "I just wanted to make sure you're okay."

"I'm fine." Her lips tingled as she looked up at him. "How's Demi?"

He raised his western hat and pushed his fingers through his short hair before he settled his hat back on his head. "She'll be all right. She just wants to believe that her mother and I will get back together someday. She wants her mother just like any girl would, I imagine."

Cat nodded, feeling a tightness in her chest as she thought of what the girl must be going through. "I sure missed my mother when she died. Even though she was an alcoholic and didn't protect me from my father. I felt like I needed her." She took a deep breath.

"My grandmother filled that spot. She was more of a mother to me than my own was."

Blake put his hands on her shoulders. "Something's wrong."

She looked down at her shoes before meeting his gaze again. "I don't think we should date. Demi doesn't need the drama at this time in her life."

He studied her for a long moment. "Demi is a big girl. She needs to understand that you're important to me."

"But—" Cat started.

"We'll keep it discreet." He searched her gaze. "I need you, Cat."

His words caused a whirling sensation in her belly. *I need you, Cat.*

She hesitated. "How could you know that so soon?"

He gave her a little smile. "I wouldn't call nineteen years soon."

"You know what I mean." She bit the inside of her lip before she continued. "We've both changed."

"And I like what I see in you." He let his hands slide down her arms to her wrists before taking her fingers in his. "You're an amazing woman, even more than the girl you were when we were together before."

She shook her head. "You can't know that."

"I can and I do." He squeezed her fingers. "Now stop arguing with me and tell me you'll go out with me Friday night."

At that moment, Friday seemed so far away. She took in a deep breath then let it out slowly. "Okay."

"Good. I'll pick you up around six in the evening if that works for you." He leaned down and kissed her again. He raised his head and smiled at her and she felt more crazy sensations pinging around in her belly.

She nodded. "That works."

He hooked his thumbs in his belt loops. "Now what about that audit?"

"Oh. The audit." She'd forgotten about it. "Do you have time for me to come by this week?"

"Right now would be nice." He gave her a slow grin.

She couldn't help a smile. "Seriously."

He shrugged. "How about Wednesday morning?"

"Demi will be at school?" Cat asked.

"Even if she wasn't, she needs to get used to you being around," he said. "But yes, she'll be at school."

"I'd rather work up to being around slowly," Cat said.

"I understand." He nodded. "I've got to get back to work. I'll see you Wednesday."

She found herself smiling. "See you then."

He kissed her, then turned and walked to his truck.

CHAPTER 12

The sound of a car driving up to the house caught Blake's attention. He tossed the last bale of alfalfa hay from the old work truck then pulled off his leather and canvas work gloves. He walked out of the barn to see a new pearl-white Cadillac he didn't recognize. He tucked the gloves into the back pocket of his Wrangler jeans and strode toward the car.

When a blonde woman in a bright red skirt and blouse stepped out of the car, Blake's jaw tensed and he had to hold back a scowl.

Sally's hair hung in long waves down her back and her cinnamon brown eyes held no smile. She wore red lipstick the same color as her dress and red high heels that weren't practical for a ranch. Not that Sally had ever been practical.

She plastered a fake smile on her beautiful face. Or at least what he had once thought of as beautiful. She had him fooled long enough for her to get pregnant and then he'd started to see her true nature. He hadn't known her well enough to see through her at the beginning. The protection they'd used hadn't worked and she got pregnant within two weeks of their meeting each other.

Even though she wasn't the kind of person he'd thought she was, he'd married her because it was the right thing to do. The six years they'd been married had been hell, but he'd tried the best he could for Demi's sake. After Sally left, he realized that the best thing for Demi was not having such an unstable person in her life.

"Sally," he said when he reached her. "What are you doing here?"

"That's some greeting." She tilted her head to the side. "Think you could find it in your heart to be kinder to the mother of your child?"

He just looked at her. "What do you need this time? Money, again?"

She kept the same pleasant expression on her face but had a spark in her eyes that might have been anger. "We need to talk. Why don't you offer me something to drink?"

"It won't be alcohol." He ignored her scowl as he strode past her and up the porch steps to the front door and he held it open for her. "I have lemonade or iced tea."

"Lemonade is fine." She followed him up the porch steps and walked in through the door he held open. He closed the door behind them. She tossed her hair over her shoulder. "I don't drink anymore."

Sure, she didn't. He didn't believe her any further than he could pitch her across the yard, which by the end of the conversation, he suspected, he would want to do.

Without answering her, he went to the kitchen, put ice in a glass, and poured her lemonade from a pitcher out of the fridge. He didn't make himself a drink.

He handed her the glass. "What brings you here?"

"I like what you've done with the place." She took the glass from him and sipped from it as she looked around the kitchen. She seemed to be taking in everything before she strolled past him into the living room. "Quite a remodel since I was here last."

"You're not here to admire the remodeling." Blake wanted to clench his teeth as he walked behind her and into the living room. "Why don't you tell me why you are here." He said the last as an order, not a question.

She faced him, determination in her brown eyes. "I want Demi to come live with me. I'm moving to the Nashville area. Maybe you can have her for the summer and some holidays."

"Like hell. You're not taking my daughter away from me, much less across the state line." He narrowed his gaze as anger began simmering beneath his skin. "You aren't a fit mother and you know it."

"I'm a perfectly fit mother." Color flamed in Sally's cheeks. "I've been out of rehab for some time now and I've been sober for six months. And, I'm getting married to a wealthy man."

Which explained the Cadillac, Blake thought.

Sally continued, "My new home is huge and will be a better environment than her living isolated with nothing but dirt and bushes around."

"No." Blake tried to keep his calm but his temper was on a

short leash. "Not happening. I have full custody and it's going to stay that way."

"A judge won't see it as you do." Sally raised her voice. "A judge will see that a daughter belongs with her mother. Demi is mine."

"A judge will see that you're not fit to care for her." Blake struggled to keep from clenching his fists at his sides and to keep his own tone down. "You're a drug addict, and an alcoholic, you can't keep a job or a home, and you abandoned your daughter eight years ago to run off with some man. No, a judge isn't going to rule in your favor."

"That's all changed." She nearly yelled the words. "I've got it together and I want my daughter."

"You think you can discard Demi then decide you want her again?" Blake's whole body was tense and he felt like putting his fist through a wall. "She's happy, stable, and she has a good life. I'm not about to let you put her through the pain you've caused her ever again."

"You won't have a choice." Sally was nearly screaming now. "My fiancé can afford to take you to court and we'll take it as far as we have to."

"Demi isn't some kind of prize for you to win." He was having a hard time not raising his own voice. "She's our daughter, not an object to fight over."

Sally sounded nearly hysterical now. "You've had her long enough. She'll be living with me now."

"Like hell," Blake ground out. "There is nothing you can do so you might as well stop it."

"Oh, yes there is," she said. "You just wait. You'll find out."

"What is that? A threat?" he said. "Are you actually threatening me?"

She sneered. "You'll learn soon enough."

"Get out," he said. "Just get out."

This time when Cat drove up to Blake's house, a late model pearl-white Cadillac was parked beside his truck. She parked her own truck on the other side of Blake's before she climbed out and headed for the house, his files tucked close to her chest in one arm.

With her opposite hand she smoothed down her flowing white eyelet skirt and adjusted her white blouse so that it was tucked in the back. She wore pretty gold flats that looked cute but wouldn't cause her to break her neck walking across the yard on a ranch.

Vaguely, she wondered who the owner of the Cadillac was. When she reached the front door, she raised her hand and knocked on the wood.

The sound of a woman shouting caused her to go still. She stood frozen on the porch, not sure what to do. Blake was clearly in the house having an argument with someone. She started to turn away to go sit in her truck when the door opened.

Blake stood in the doorway, his jaw tight but his expression relaxing a little when he saw her. "Come on in."

She cleared her throat. "Sounds like you're busy."

"It's fine." He stepped back so that she could come in.

Cat hesitated but then walked in to see a furious blonde with bright red lipstick standing in the living room. She wore a tiny red skirt, her breasts were large with her generous cleavage showing in the V of her red button-up blouse. The woman's hands were propped on her hips and fire was in her eyes. She was beautiful—

and she looked a lot like Demi. This had to be Sally, Blake's ex.

"Sally," Blake said, confirming her suspicions, "this is Cat." He turned to her and gestured to the woman. "This is my ex-wife, Sally."

"Cat?" the woman spat before Blake could make introductions. "You're the one who dumped him and broke his poor little 'ol heart?"

Cat hugged the files to her like a shield. "I'm his accountant."

"And my girlfriend." Blake settled his hand on her shoulder. "Do you want to wait in the office, Cat?"

Surprised that he'd introduced her as his girlfriend, she just nodded. She wanted out of there as fast as possible.

"Don't go. I'm leaving," Sally said to Cat. Her sneer made her far from beautiful as she turned to Blake. "I can see you're going to be busy with Scarface."

Cat felt like she'd been slapped. Blake's features hardened. He went to the door, opened it, and stood to the side. "Call next time you want to talk about Demi. Don't feel the need to stop by again."

"I'm going to get her back." Sally snapped the words. "Don't try and stop me because you're going to lose her."

Blake pointed out the open door.

Sally marched past him, stopped to glare at Cat, then walked through the doorway.

Blake quietly but firmly closed the door behind the woman.

When the door was shut he went to Cat and took her in his arms. "I'm sorry."

"You have nothing to apologize for," she said against his shirt.

"What she said to you." He kissed the top of her head. "I can only say, I'm sorry."

"It's all right." Cat tried for a smile as she stepped away from him, but the smile felt tight and artificial. "It's not the first time I've been called that."

"Oh, honey." He took her into his arms again and held her close like he was never going to let her go.

He rocked her in his strong arms and she found herself sinking into his embrace and breathing in the clean smell of his T-shirt and his masculine scent.

This time when they parted she raised file folders. "We have work to do."

He shook his head but put his arm around her shoulders and headed with her down the hall to his office.

When they walked through the door, she saw his desk and thought of the way he'd taken her there. Papers flying everywhere as he buried himself inside her.

Feeling warmth flooding her, she glanced up at him.

He gave her a sexy little grin. Even though she hadn't said anything out loud, he said, "Me, too. I'll never look at my desk the same way again."

She smiled back at him. "I'd have to say that was the most exciting client meeting I've ever had."

CHAPTER 13

"And I'm the only client you'll ever have that kind of meeting with." The expression in Blake's eyes told Cat that he meant it.

She didn't bristle at the near command in his words. Instead, she felt giddy inside, his near demand making her feel as if she belonged to him. It surprised her how much she liked that feeling.

He took the file folders from her and set them aside on his desk before bringing her into his arms and kissing her. His kiss was slow and passionate, sending shivers of desire through her.

When he raised his head he trailed his fingers from her eyes to her hair and back. "Such beautiful cat's eyes," he murmured. "I've always loved your eyes."

She ran her finger along the front of his shirt. "Don't we need to get to work, Mr. McBride?"

"I have a few things in mind that I'd like to take care of first."
His smile was entirely sexual. "Unless you have other plans, Ms.
Hayden?"

"Whatever you require, I'm here to help." She realized her
breathing was coming quicker. "The client is always in charge."

"You've got that right." He cupped her ass and caught her off
guard as he raised her up. She wrapped her arms around his neck
and clenched her thighs around his trim hips. He was so muscular
and strong that she felt like a doll in his arms.

He turned toward the door and started carrying her out of the
office and down the hall. "Hey." She laughed as she clung to him,
her arms tighter around his neck. "We're supposed to be working."

"I've got another project in mind." He gripped her close so
that she could feel his belt buckle through her skirt. And that
wasn't all she could feel. "Now shush before I throw you over my
shoulder and spank you for talking back."

She tilted her chin. "You wouldn't dare, Mr. McBride."

He raised a brow. "Are you challenging me?"

She shook her head then squealed as he hefted her over his
shoulder, her face against his back and her ass in the air. He pushed
up her flowing skirt so that it hung over her back and he ran his
hand over her pink silk panties.

"Blake!" she shouted as he landed the first swat on her ass.
He swatted her hard enough that tears wet her eyes and her rear
stung. "No fair."

"You dared me." He continued walking down the hall. "I only
took you up on it. I'd say that's more than fair."

She remembered the old days when they used to dare each
other and the fun they'd had. Him carrying her over his shoulder

and spanking her was a first, though.

He spanked her again and she shouted out from the pain of his big hand against her bottom. There was something erotic about being spanked like this that turned her on more than she could have imagined.

He walked through the door to the master bedroom, swatted her a third time, then shut and locked the door behind them. Even though they were home alone, she guessed he wasn't taking any chances.

While she was still over his shoulder, he slipped his hand beneath her panties and stroked the soft skin of her ass before sliding his finger into her folds, catching her by surprise.

"You're already wet," he murmured as he stroked her clit. "I love that."

She gasped, her eyes widening as he moved his finger, drawing out more of her desire. If he kept that up, she was going to come before they even got started.

He slipped his finger out then let her slide down his body so that they were facing each other. Her nipples rubbed hard against his chest as he brought her down. This time he didn't rip off her buttons. Instead he unbuttoned them one at a time until her blouse fell away, revealing the pink satin bra she wore.

"Mmmm." He ran his finger over the curve above her breast. "Matches your panties."

She let the blouse slide down her arms and he caught it and tossed it on a chair. She slipped off her shoes and stood in her bare feet as he pushed her skirt over her hips and let it fall to the floor. She stepped out of it and he laid it on the chair, too.

"My little KitCat," he murmured as she stood in front of him.

He slid his fingers into her dark hair, massaging her scalp, making her sigh with pleasure. He slipped his fingers from her hair and grasped her by her shoulders and brought her close for a long, luxurious kiss.

When he drew away, she looked up into his beautiful green eyes. His features were almost harsh but he was gorgeous to her.

"You are the most precious woman I know." He gave her a soft kiss on the corner of her mouth. "You don't know how much I've missed you." He moved his lips down her throat to the curve of her neck and shoulder. "Hell, I didn't even realize how much I missed you."

"I've thought about you a lot over the years." She found it hard to talk as he kissed her shoulder while pulling her bra straps aside and letting them slide down her arms. "One of my biggest regrets was leaving you."

"Shhh…" He made the soft sound as he kissed her shoulder. He rose and met her gaze again. "Everything we've been through in life has brought us to this very moment. I don't intend to waste the time we have now."

"Yes." She reached up and kissed him and he returned it with a rumbling groan.

He reached behind her and unfastened her bra before sliding it the rest of the way down and letting it drop to the floor. Her breasts seemed to fascinate him as he cupped them and circled her nipples with his thumbs. She grasped his shoulders as he lowered his head and flicked his tongue over her nipples before sucking each of them and she could barely keep her knees from giving out. Knowing just how much she loved having her nipples played with, he gave them extra time and attention.

When he got down on one knee, she slipped her hands into his short hair and felt his scalp beneath her fingertips. He tugged her panties down to her ankles and she stepped out of them.

"Now I'm naked and you still have all of your clothes on," she said as he got to his feet. "What are we going to do about that?"

"Maybe I'm going to take you just like this." He gave her a sexy grin. "Bend you over that trunk and fuck you now." He gestured to a large trunk with a domed lid at the foot of his bed.

The thought of him taking her like that caused an even greater ache between her thighs. She almost dared him to, but she wanted him naked.

She started with the top button of his western work shirt and worked her way down to where his shirt was tucked into his jeans. She pulled it out and pushed his shirt over his shoulders, which left his muscular torso as her playing field.

"My, how you've grown." She tilted her head up to smile at him as she smoothed her palms over his chest, up to his shoulders, then back down to his six pack. She looked back at his beautiful body. She loved the way the veins stood out on his arms as they flexed. The power in him seem barely controlled as she touched him. "You always had a great body, but you're a god now." She smiled at him and cupped his cock through his jeans. "Yes, you're a big boy."

He gave a low chuckle. "All you want me for is my body."

She grinned. "And I intend to have it."

The corner of his mouth quirked. "Then I'd better get these boots off."

She pushed him back onto the bed. "I'll do it."

He sat on the edge of the bed and watched her breasts bounce as she grasped his boot at the heel and levered it off before discarding it. She pulled off the sock and dropped it on the boot. She caressed his bare foot and watched him as he kept his eyes fixed on her, his gaze traveling over her face to her breasts and to the patch of hair at the apex of her thighs. The hard ridge of his erection was obvious behind the tough cotton of his jeans.

After she'd removed his other boot, she took his hand and tugged him so that he got back to his feet. His eyes were dark as he watched her, letting her take control.

She grasped his belt buckle. "Now to unwrap the rest of you."

CHAPTER 14

Blake's cock ached so damned bad he wanted to get out of these jeans, throw Cat over that old trunk, and fuck her until both of them were cross-eyed.

But, he wanted to take it slow and easy with her this time. He wanted to make love to her, taste her, caress her. He didn't have any idea of how he was going to control himself with her.

She pushed his hands away when he started to help her undress him. "I want to do it," she said. "Let me."

"Cat," he said in a warning tone. "You'd better be careful."

She just smiled up at him.

He clenched his hands at his sides to control himself as she unbuckled his belt and then her warm fingers were unbuttoning his jeans and drawing down his zipper. She skimmed her knuckles over his erection and he sucked in his breath

It took too damned much time for her to push his jeans down along with his boxer briefs. When he stepped out of them, he prepared to bring her to her feet but she grasped his cock in one hand and his balls in her other. He wasn't going anywhere.

She smiled up at him, her golden brown eyes meeting his. He held his breath as she lowered her head and slipped her mouth over his cock. He groaned as she brought him all the way to the back of her throat.

"Damn, KitCat," he managed to say. "You always could drive me crazy."

Her eyes glittered as she moved her head up and down in a slow pace, teasing him with her lips and tongue as she sucked him.

Even though she wanted to be in control, he couldn't keep his hands off of her. He slipped his fingers into her hair and found himself holding her head still as he moved his hips so that he was gently thrusting into her mouth. She moved one hand on his cock in time with her movements as her other hand fondled and squeezed his balls. She squeezed them so hard that he felt a moment of pain that mingled with the pleasure of her mouth on him.

She made soft sounds of delight as she sucked and licked him. He watched his cock moving in and out of her mouth as she stared up at him and he felt one hell of an orgasm building inside of him. He planned to take her on the bed and he didn't intend to come in her mouth. But right now, it felt so damned good.

When it became more than he could take, he held her head still and drew his cock out of her mouth.

"You've got to stop, honey," he said when he saw her disappointed gaze. "I have too much planned to end it this fast."

"You taste so good," she said as he brought her to her feet.

He kissed her, a long and lingering kiss.

Cat's belly swooped as Blake swept her into his arms and caught her up to him. She loved the feel of his powerful body as he carried her to the bed. He set her gently in the middle of the king-sized bed on the soft comforter and slipped onto the mattress beside her.

He propped himself on his forearm and stroked the side of her face almost reverently. "I can't believe you're back here, beside me." He moved his fingers into her hair before lowering his mouth to hers and kissing her.

Morning light fell across them through the open blinds, the warmth of the sunshine seeming to raise her already elevated temperature.

She wanted him so badly, but at the same time she loved the way he was taking it slow with her, the way he looked at her.

"You have the same good heart, the same beauty within, that always attracted me to you." He kissed the corner of her mouth. "We've each lived a lifetime separately. But you're still the same sweet woman you were when we were together. And I'm still the same man who never stopped loving you."

Her eyes widened as she looked up at him. She wasn't sure what to say. So much had happened over the years. Despite what he'd said, she didn't think she was the same person he thought she was. Would he still love her if he got to know her better?

Before she could speak, he put his fingers to her lips. "Shhh... Don't say anything. Not yet."

While he held her gaze, he moved his palm along her body

then skimmed the back of his hand over her nipples, causing her to gasp with pleasure. He trailed his fingers down her flat abdomen to the soft curls at the apex of her thighs.

She shivered with want and need, but something more, too. Her heart was filled with whatever was rising inside her. It filled to overflowing, a warmth that suffused her entire being. How could she be so blessed as to be in Blake's arms again after she'd left the way she did?

He moved his fingers back to her face and she stilled as he traced the scar from one side of her face to the other. "You must have been through so much, honey." He cupped her scarred cheek. "I wish I could have been there for you."

The beauty of the moment made tears back up behind her eyes. How could she have left this man?

"You're so beautiful." He kissed her scarred cheek before moving his lips down the slender column of her neck to the hollow at the base of her throat. "Everything about you is beautiful."

The way he accepted her, the way he told her she was beautiful, filled her heart even more to the brim.

He trailed kisses to the valley between her breasts and then she arched her back as he took one of her nipples in his mouth and rolled the other between his thumb and forefinger. As he licked and sucked each of her nipples she squirmed and grasped his powerful shoulders like she was clinging to a life preserver to keep from drowning in ecstasy.

When he moved his mouth to her bellybutton, his big hands felt calloused and rough against her soft skin as he slid them beneath her ass. He eased lower, his lips and tongue leaving a damp trail down to the curls below.

He moved his big shoulders between her thighs, spreading them wide. She still couldn't get over how big he was now. He was the same Blake, but even more powerful and rugged than he'd been when they'd been together as teenagers.

She tensed as he kissed the inside of one thigh and then the other and she waited for his mouth to move to her folds. His hands beneath her ass brought her closer to him. And she heard his deep inhalation.

Her heart beat faster as he spread her thighs even wider, lowered his head and ran his tongue along her folds.

She hissed with pleasure. He continued to lick her clit and she realized she was grabbing the comforter to either side of her and clenching it in her fists as if to ground herself. She wanted to toss her head back and revel in the sensations, but she wanted to watch him, too.

Seeing him between her thighs, looking at her while he licked her, nearly made her come unglued. Incredible sensations built inside her and she felt like her whole body was whirling and she couldn't control anything. She wanted to hold back, to draw it out. But when he slid two fingers into her core and started pumping them in and out, she couldn't stop herself from falling apart.

She couldn't have held back the scream if she'd tried. She thrashed beneath the assault of his mouth and fingers as he continued drawing out her orgasm.

When he raised his head, his eyes were dark with satisfaction. He moved up her body and braced himself above her so that his full weight wasn't on her. They'd already talked about safe sex the second time they were together that first night and the fact that he didn't need a condom.

"Take me, Blake." She found herself begging when he just stayed still and watched her. "Please."

She reached between them and grasped his cock, putting it at the entrance to her core. He kept his gaze pinned to hers as he pushed himself into her.

Her eyes widened at the feel of his thickness and length filling her up. Every time he entered her felt like the first time.

He began a slow and easy pace as he continued to watch her. His jaw grew tense as he moved and her breathing grew harsher, perspiration coating her skin and his.

"You're so damned beautiful, KitCat," he murmured and she felt the truth in his words. He made her feel beautiful and sexy again.

"I want to come when you do." She remembered all the times they would reach orgasm together and the sense of completeness it had always given her.

He nodded and moved in and out, picking up his pace. She felt herself spiraling, an orgasm so near, she could barely keep from coming.

"I'm there," she whispered. "I'm waiting for you."

He thrust a few times more. "Come, baby. Come now."

She cried out with the exquisite pleasure that took hold of her as his shout joined hers. He continued moving in and out as her body vibrated. She felt the throb of his cock inside her as her core contracted around him, drawing out his semen to fill her.

He stopped and lowered his head, still braced above her, his chest rising and falling with his harsh breaths. He was still inside her and she loved the feel of him there. Then he pulled out and caught her to him as he rolled onto his back and brought her on top of him.

She laughed as she found herself above him, her skin slick against his, her long hair sliding against his skin and brushing his face. He looked at her as if she might be some kind of goddess that he'd captured and intended to keep forever, even if he had to lock her away.

He cupped the back of her head and brought her down for a long kiss. When their lips parted, he pushed her hair behind her ear. "I wish we could stay here all day, with you in my arms."

She smiled down at him. "We have work to do."

He rolled her onto her back, causing her to giggle. "Not if I keep you prisoner."

She laughed and looped her arms around his neck. "That might not be such a bad fate."

He grinned. "Just know that I don't intend to let you go." His expression grew more serious and she knew that he meant it when he said, "Ever."

Happiness like she hadn't felt in a long time filled her, completed her. Where once she'd felt broken, now she felt whole again.

It was a long time before they made it out of bed and back to reality.

CHAPTER 15

Cat waited at Folsom Ranch for the last couple of 4-H'ers in the horse club to arrive. One of those who hadn't shown up yet was Demi, and Cat hoped she'd make it. She was surprised at the flutters in her belly as she prayed that the girl would be accepting of her. It was important to her in a way she didn't fully understand.

It was a beautiful May Saturday with a nice breeze that smelled of dust, horses, and the scent of the oncoming summer that always started early in Arizona. Cat's western hat shaded her eyes from the rising sun.

The horses—Gretchen, Dolly, and Shelton—stood beside her, saddled, swatting away flies from their rumps with their long tails. Two of the 4-H'ers had ridden their own horses over.

Cat thought about her time with Blake over the past few days.

After spending Wednesday morning in bed before getting to work on the audit, they'd seen each other twice more during the week.

Friday they'd played putt-putt golf and had laughed like teenagers and Cat had fallen into a fit of giggles when Blake had hit his ball across the course, in the wrong direction, and had made a hole-in-one at the Dutch windmill instead of in the castle that had been directly in front of them.

Cat held back a grin as she saw Blake's red truck when came around a bend in the road and Amy said, "Demi's here."

For some reason, Brett looked like he wanted to hide as Blake brought the truck to a stop and parked.

Both Demi and Blake climbed out of the truck and Cat's belly fluttered for an entirely different reason than when she'd been worried about seeing Demi. Cat felt like she could never get enough of looking at him and having him close. When he reached them she was glad he didn't kiss her in front of the kids and Demi. He just gave her a smile that sent thrills through her from the top of her head to the tips of her toes.

Demi, on the other hand, had her arms crossed over her chest and wouldn't meet Cat's eyes. Cat nearly sighed. At least the girl wasn't glaring at her.

Blake went up to Brett who looked at him with something like fear. Blake held out his hand and Brett took it hesitantly. When they released their grip, Blake spoke quietly to the boy but Cat couldn't hear him nor Brett's response. But when they parted, the boy looked relieved and even smiled.

Demi had tensed and had been watching with what had looked like concern, but she visibly relaxed when she saw Brett smile.

Blake squeezed Demi's shoulder then touched his hat with one hand when he looked at Cat. "I'll be back to pick up Demi when you're ready." He looked at the girl. "Call me when it's time."

She nodded. "Okay, Dad."

Cat did her best not to stare after Blake and admire his nice ass and the way he filled out his western shirt and his Wranglers as he walked away.

Apparently, she hadn't done a very good job of hiding her interest because Demi was staring at her when she turned her gaze back to the group.

"As you know, the Flagstaff Junior Rodeo is in two weeks." Cat smiled at the 4-H'ers standing around her. "We're going to pack in as much practice as possible between now and then."

The teens nodded and started talking about who their competition was from the surrounding counties. Unanimously, the kids said Demi was the top barrel racer and Brett was the best at tie-down calf roping. The other 4-H'ers were strong competitors as well.

Demi acted like a pro when it came to participating in the discussions, even when it meant talking to Cat. She was certain, though, that Demi was still unhappy about the relationship between her father and Cat. She could only hope the girl came around and that it wouldn't take too long—that was, if she ever did.

But Cat wasn't ready to look that far into the future. What was between her and Blake was incredible, but would it last? Would he stop finding her attractive as time passed?

Cat gave tips and guidance as the 4-H'ers practiced their events. They would need to practice a lot on their own horses between now and the rodeo.

When it was time for Demi to practice her event, she mounted Gretchen and hesitated. She looked down from where she sat on the horse. "Will you teach me that trick again, the one that you showed me at the last meeting?"

"Sure." Cat felt a little sense of elation that Demi was turning to her for something. She mounted Dolly and the horses moved side by side as Cat went over the move that had helped her to win several championships. "Watch me now."

Demi sat on Gretchen and watched Cat ride to the starting point on Dolly. Cat felt a sense of elation as she prepared to race Dolly. Even though she wasn't going to go full out, the pure enjoyment of the moment made her heart thrum.

She raced the barrels, wishing she could run them hard. No matter her insistence on riding horses, a niggling fear was always at the back of her mind that it was possible for her to take a spill and hit her head.

When she finished the cloverleaf pattern and trotted up to Demi and Gretchen, Cat felt a flush in her cheeks and couldn't help the broad smile on her face.

"You love it, don't you," Demi said in a way that sounded like a statement, not question. "Just like me."

Cat grinned. "Absolutely. As a 4-H leader, these last couple of meetings are the first time I've been back at it since the accident and it feels good to be doing what I loved, even if it's only in a small way." She was surprised that she was talking so animatedly with Demi, as if there was nothing between them.

Demi seemed to have a hard time keeping from smiling, too. Regardless of Demi's feelings about Cat and her dad being together, this was a bond they both shared. Cat hoped it would be enough for them to develop the start of a relationship. It wouldn't be enough to sustain it, but it was a start.

"I'd better get going." Demi took off on Gretchen and trotted to the starting point.

When Demi was ready, Cat shouted for her to go and timed her. The girl was poetry in motion, her movements smooth and beautiful. Even though Gretchen wasn't her own horse, it was like the pair of them had been practicing together forever.

"Beautiful," Cat said, when Demi returned, and the other teens clapped and called out to her.

Demi's face looked as flushed as Cat's had felt and her eyes glittered with happiness as she grinned. Cat knew the feeling. The girl felt more at home on a horse than anywhere else.

Cat and Demi rode side-by-side back to the group and both dismounted.

"Two more weeks." Amy bounced up and down on her boot heels. "I can't wait." She whispered to Demi, "Maybe that cute guy from Coconino County will be there. Clive Turner." Amy giggled after she said it and Demi grinned.

Cat hid a smile and talked to the group. "We'll meet again next Saturday, same time, same place. Can everyone make it?"

The kids nodded and said they'd be there. Brett and Demi volunteered to take the three horses to the barn and put them up. The rest of 4-H'ers left as their parents arrived and the two who had come by horseback left the same way.

Blake's red truck came up the drive and Cat smiled as he pulled up and parked. When he walked up to Cat, he looked around, didn't see anyone, and gave her a quick kiss.

"How about dinner tonight?" he asked. "My house."

She brushed back hair that had blown into her face. "Are you sure that's wise, with Demi?"

He nodded. "She needs to get used to you being around."

Cat smiled at the thought of being with Blake at his home. She liked being there with him. "I'd like that."

"Good." He gave her a light kiss. "Is Demi in the barn?"

"With Brett." Cat nodded. "Putting up the horses."

Blake frowned. He started toward the barn and she jogged to keep up with him.

"What's wrong?" she asked.

"Maybe nothing," he said beneath his breath. "I hope."

As they walked through the huge door, Cat blinked as her eyes adjusted to the dimness of the barn, smells of alfalfa and manure meeting her nose.

Her gaze fell on Brett and Demi—and they were kissing.

Blake made a low growling noise and strode toward the pair.

Demi squealed with surprise and jumped away from Brett the moment she saw her father. The boy looked terrified.

When Blake reached the pair, he put his hand on Demi's shoulder.

"Dad, no," Demi said. "Don't get mad."

"Stay away from my daughter." Blake's voice was deadly calm as he spoke to Brett. "I never want to see you alone with Demi again."

Brett's throat worked as he said, "Yes, sir."

"We're going home." Blake guided Demi, his hand still on her shoulder. Tears filled the girl's eyes.

Demi broke into a run and raced out of the barn. Through the barn doors, Cat saw that Demi reached Blake's truck before he did. She climbed into the passenger seat and slammed the door shut.

Blake looked over his shoulder at Cat. "Six, tonight," he said and she nodded before he turned and headed toward the truck again.

Cat faced Brett who looked like he'd just escaped being executed. "What in the world were you thinking?" she said. "First of all, you're sixteen and she's fourteen. Secondly, this is a 4-H club where you're here to practice and learn. It's not some place for you to make out with a girl two years younger than you."

He hung his head. "I'm sorry."

"Demi's father is the one you're going to need to apologize to," Cat said. "Now, run along and I'll finish taking care of the horses."

Brett nodded and left the barn, leaving Cat behind, shaking her head. She wouldn't want to be Demi or Blake right now.

CHAPTER 16

Cat stood at Blake's front door, waiting a moment before she rapped her knuckles on the wood. She felt a little jittery. She shouldn't be nervous about being accepted by a teenager, but she was. She liked Demi and wanted the girl to like her as well but she understood if Demi didn't want to accept her. The girl had had her father to herself all of these years and wasn't ready to share.

The night was cool, the air fresh and clean. Cat wore comfortable Wrangler jeans and a sleeveless white western blouse with one of her several pairs of boots. Her long black hair was pulled back in a French braid and she wore light makeup. She held a pan of apple crumble in one arm.

Just as she raised her free hand to knock, the door opened. Blake stood in the doorway and he smiled when he saw her and held the door open so that she could walk in. When he'd closed the door behind her, he lowered his head and gave her a lingering kiss.

She looked past him. "Where's Demi?"

"Still in her room." He sighed and shook his head. "This time I don't know how long it's going to take her to get past this."

Cat thought for a moment. "Can I talk to her? We seemed to have connected a little today at the meeting."

Blake rubbed his hand through his short hair. "She's also sulking because I took away her phone and she's not too happy about having you over for dinner."

"It might be good for us to talk things over," Cat said.

"Yeah. Maybe she needs a female to talk with." He gestured down the hall. "Last door on the right."

"I made apple crumble." She handed him the pan. "I remember how you used to like it."

He smiled. "You remember right."

"I'll talk to Demi now." Cat bit her lower lip as she walked down the hall and paused in front of the door that was cracked open. She took a deep breath and knocked lightly on the wood. "Demi?"

"What do you want?" came the sullen reply.

"Can I come in for a moment?" Cat asked.

"Whatever," Demi muttered.

Cat grasped the handle and opened the door the rest of the way. Demi was sitting on her bed with her arms wrapped around her knees, which were drawn to her chest. She rested her chin on her knees.

Demi didn't look at Cat as she sat on the bed next to the girl. Both were silent for a few moments.

"Why are you here?" Demi said, still not looking at Cat.

Cat watched the girl. "I want to talk with you."

"Everything was fine before you showed up." Demi crossed her arms over her chest. "You're just going to come between me and Dad."

Cat shook her head. "Nothing will ever put me between you and your father."

"Right," Demi said sarcastically. "You already are."

"Your father loves you," Cat said quietly. "Nothing will ever change that."

Demi shifted on the bed. "If he loves me, why won't he let me date?"

Cat was a little surprised at the switch in conversation. "He just doesn't want anything to happen to you."

"He doesn't want me to grow up." Demi stared at the wall. "He wants me to stay a little girl forever."

"Brett is a sixteen-year-old boy," Cat said.

Demi scowled. "That's only two years between us."

Cat studied the girl. "At your age, that's a big difference."

"Not that big," Demi grumbled.

"Yes, it is." Cat wanted the girl to understand. "Boys that age are on the cusp of manhood. You're a young woman but you still need some time to grow up."

"What do you know?" Demi turned her glare on Cat. "You're not even a mother."

Cat felt the familiar ache and pain grip her as the words cut into her heart. For a moment she couldn't talk. "I was," she said in a near whisper.

Demi frowned and cut her gaze to Cat. "Did you leave your

kid like my mom left me?"

Cat shook her head and tried to hold back tears. "Melanie died when she was four. She would have been your age now."

A stunned look crossed Demi's face and she looked ashamed and sorrowful all at once. "I'm sorry, Cat. That was mean of me. I'm sorry you lost your daughter."

Despite trying her best not to cry, a tear rolled down Cat's cheek. "I miss her." She pushed the tear away with her fingertips. "When I tell you that I think you're too young to be with a boy that old, I'm thinking how I would have felt about my own daughter in that situation."

"How did Melanie die?" Demi asked quietly.

"Leukemia." Cat looked at her fingers in her lap. "She developed it when she was two and was sick most of her young life." Cat took a deep, shuddering breath. "It seemed like I barely got to know her and love her and then she was gone." She gave a sad smile. "But I still think she's an angel watching over me."

Demi slipped her feet out from under her and let them hang over the edge of the bed. She scooted closer to Cat so that they were shoulder to shoulder. "I'm really sorry," Demi said again.

Cat turned her head and looked at the girl beside her and did her best to smile. "I think she might have been like you when she grew up. She was a pretty girl with long dark hair and a sweet smile. Toward the end she lost all of her hair but she was still beautiful."

"If she looked like you, she would have been beautiful," Demi said as she looked at Cat.

Without thinking, Cat touched the scar on the cheek it crossed.

"The scar doesn't make any difference." Demi's expression

was sincere. "I hardly notice it."

"Thank you." Cat gave a soft smile. "I don't know if I'm any good at this since my daughter was so small and you're a young woman. But I can tell you how I would feel. I would be just as protective as your father is."

Demi swung her feet from where she sat perched on the edge of the bed. "He won't let me date until I'm sixteen."

"That's a good age to start," Cat said. "But he lets you go out with groups of friends which includes guys and girls right?"

Demi picked at a fold on the knee of her jeans. "Yes, but Amy's allowed to go on supervised dates now and she's the same age as me."

Cat thought about that for a moment. "Maybe your dad would allow that if you wanted to date a boy your own age."

With her head tilted to the side, Demi seemed to think about it. "I don't know if I want Dad on a date with me. That would be too weird."

Cat held back a smile. "Think about it and talk to your dad."

"I like Brett, though." Demi looked up at Cat. "I mean I *really* like him."

"It's not easy being a teenager." Cat crossed her boots at her ankles. "Even when I was sixteen my grandmother didn't want me to date your father and we were the same age."

"It's hard to think of you and Dad as teenagers and boyfriend and girlfriend." Demi frowned. "It's hard to think of you and Dad dating now, too."

"I can understand that," Cat said.

"So you really care about my dad?" Demi asked.

"I care for your father more than even I could have imagined."

Cat stared at a poster of a blue-eyed paint horse on the wall. "I loved him so much when we were teenagers. I've never felt anything like that in my life."

"And you love him now," Demi said.

After a moment, Cat gave a slow nod. "A love like that...I don't think it can ever go away."

Demi studied Cat. "Then, why did you leave him?"

"My father was abusive and I wanted to get out of Prescott and as far away from him as I could go." Cat sighed and stared at her boots. "Your dad didn't want to leave—all of his family is here. I was young and so full of emotion and pain that I ran the first chance I got." She'd used Toby as a way to escape her father.

"That's sad about your father." Demi was frowning. "He was a mean man?"

"Very. I wasn't as lucky as you," Cat said. "One of the reasons I ended up in rodeo is because I'd go to the neighbors and they'd let me ride their horses and train there. It was an escape for me, and horses and rodeo grew to be loves like no other in my life." She paused. "Of course I loved them in a different way than I'd loved your dad."

"Why did you come back now?" Demi asked.

"My grandmother is ill." Cat felt a heavy weight press down on her. "I want to be with her as much as I can during her remaining months and hopefully, years."

A light rap came on the doorframe. Demi tensed a little as she looked up and saw Blake standing in the doorway.

He looked from Demi to Cat and smiled. "Dinner's ready, girls."

"We'll be right there," Cat said.

"Don't take too long. Dinner will get cold." He turned away and left.

"Your dad is a good man." Cat smiled. "You know that."

"Inside, I know he wants what's best for me." Demi tugged at the fold in her jeans. "It's just hard sometimes."

"I wish I'd had a dad like yours," Cat said. "My life would have been a lot different than it turned out to be."

"You never would have left Prescott then," Demi said.

Cat thought about it for a moment. "Maybe things worked out the way they were supposed to and are now coming full circle. I would never have had Melanie and your dad wouldn't have had you. You are two blessings who were meant to be."

"I think you're right," Demi said.

"We'd better go." Cat pushed herself up from the mattress to her feet. "Something smells wonderful and I'd hate for it to get cold."

Demi nodded and stood then met Cat's gaze. "Thank you, Cat."

Cat wanted to reach out and tuck a stray hair that had escaped Demi's braid but she held herself back.

Instead she smiled and they walked out the door toward the kitchen.

CHAPTER 17

Sunday morning, Blake stood on his front porch as he looked at the caller ID on his cell phone and frowned. He wasn't in the mood to talk with Sally and deal with her antagonism, but he wasn't one to ignore calls or delay in facing anything that came his way.

Last night had turned out well with Demi seeming to have come to terms with Blake's rule against dating, especially older boys. Although appearing wary at times, his daughter also seemed to be more accepting of Cat.

But now he had to deal with Sally.

"Sally," he answered.

"I'm taking Demi when school gets out for the summer," Sally stated the moment he answered. "Permanently."

He'd had just about all he could take of Sally and her insistence that she was taking Demi from him. "We've been through this. You're not taking her."

"She's not yours." Something like satisfaction rang in Sally's voice.

A bad feeling that came out of nowhere washed over him. "She's my daughter and she's staying with me. You're not fit to be a mother."

"You're not her biological father." Sally sounded triumphant. "She wasn't really a month early. I was two weeks pregnant when I picked you out to be the father of my child and screwed you."

Cold crept over his skin and a sick sensation shot through his gut. "Stop playing games. This is our daughter's life."

"It's no game," Sally said in a too-sweet voice. "The man who got me pregnant didn't have a dime. You're a McBride and I knew you had money, so I went where the money was."

Heat burned over Blake's skin. "I don't know what in the hell you're up to, but you're not getting my daughter."

"*My* daughter," Sally said. "Don't you wonder why she doesn't look like you? She's not your daughter. She's mine."

"Bullshit," Blake said, but he felt like his mind was spinning. Was she telling the truth?

"You don't want to do it the easy way?" Sally said. "Fine. You won't have her at all. No visitation. None."

Blake clenched his hands at his sides. "I've had it with your games, Sally."

"You're the reason I had problems to begin with," Sally went on. "I wouldn't have turned to drugs and alcohol if it weren't for you." Her voice rose. "She wants to live with me anyway. You're too strict and she's unhappy. I'll take care of her and she'll have a beautiful house and not live out in the sticks."

"This conversation has gone far enough," Blake said.

"You've got a few more weeks with her," Sally went on. "That'll give her time to get together what she needs, and you can make your goodbyes."

Blake noticed a vehicle tearing down the road, its tires kicking up clouds of dust as it sped toward the ranch.

"I have full custody of Demi and you're not taking her anywhere." Blake's heart was thudding harder. "As far as paternity, that's nothing but bullshit."

"You'll find out real soon that it's not," she said in a voice that sickened his stomach.

Was she telling the truth? Or was this another one of her ploys?

The car that had been speeding down the road came through the main gate and then parked in front of the house.

"I don't have time for this." He started toward the car where a man was getting out. "I've got things to do."

"Did someone get there just now?" she asked innocently.

Blake held back a scowl as a man wearing slacks and a button-up shirt strode toward him, dust covering his shoes as he walked across the hard-packed dirt driveway.

A sinking feeling weighted his gut as the man held out two envelopes. Blake took them and the man said, "You've been served," and then walked back to the car.

"What perfect timing," Sally said over the phone, obviously hearing the man and knowing all along that he'd been on his way. "That's a court order for a paternity test, and an order for Demi to be tested, too."

The rest of whatever she said was a buzz in his ears. He disconnected the call without telling her goodbye and shoved the phone into its holster on his belt.

He barely noticed his hands were trembling as he opened one of the two envelopes. He unfolded the papers and saw that it was exactly what she'd said it was. An order for a paternity test. He opened the second envelope. An order for Demi to have her blood tested.

He sat heavily in one of the chairs on the front porch and covered his eyes with his hand, elbow resting on his thigh. Was it true? Was Demi some other man's biological child and Sally would be able to take her away?

Blake hadn't cried since he was a kid but he felt an ache behind his eyes now. He couldn't lose Demi. She was his daughter. No matter what the paternity test might say, Demi was *his* daughter.

He gritted his teeth, wanting to shred the document and burn the scraps to ash.

Over and over in his mind he turned the thought around that Demi might not be his. He couldn't get himself to believe it was true and that he could lose his daughter.

He didn't give a damn what the paternity test came up with. Demi was his daughter and he'd fight for her. He wasn't letting her go.

An odd sensation had been floating in Cat's belly all morning as she took care of chores and prepared to go to Grandma Hayden's. Cat had no idea what was making her feel this way, but she felt unnerved.

She always spent Sundays with her grandmother, but she had the strangest feeling that Blake needed her. She pulled her cell phone out of her pocket and looked at it for a moment. Last night had been great with Blake and Demi and the only feelings that had lingered were good ones. So why did she feel like something was off?

She went to her list of contacts and called Blake. It rang a few times.

"Hi, honey." Blake's voice had a forced edge to it.

"Is everything all right?" she asked with hesitation.

He paused. "I don't know."

She realized she was holding her breath and let it out in a slow exhale. "Do you want to talk about it?"

"Yeah," he said. "But not on the phone."

"Do you want to come to Grandma Hayden's for supper?" Cat felt another nervous flutter in her belly. "She'd love to have company and I know she'd be happy to see you."

He paused again and his hesitation made her feel more concerned. "Would she mind if Demi came?"

"She'd be thrilled to have Demi visit." Cat started pacing her small kitchen. "She said something about having prepared some kind of chicken casserole for today and she always makes enough for a family even though it's usually just the two of us. I know there will be plenty because I end up taking a ton of leftovers home. I think she's making a red velvet cake, too."

"Your granny makes the best red velvet cake," he said. "What time?"

She glanced at the time on the microwave. It was almost noon. "Grandma likes to have an early supper. How about coming over around four and we'll have supper at five?"

"Four it is." He still sounded like something was wrong and it made her tense inside. "Granny's still in the same place?"

"Yes." Cat nodded to herself. "I'll see you then."

After they disconnected, she called Grandma Hayden to let her know that Blake and Demi were coming. Like Cat had expected, her grandmother was thrilled.

It was close to noon when Cat arrived at her Grandma Hayden's. Like Cat had expected, her grandmother was smiling and humming as she busied herself around the house. Cat gave Grandma a kiss and helped her wherever she was needed. The elderly woman seemed happier and in less pain than usual.

A couple of minutes after four there was a knock and Cat opened the door to greet Blake and Demi. After Cat said hello to Demi, Blake gave Cat a light kiss. Demi watched and her brow furrowed. It didn't look like she approved, but she didn't say anything.

Grandma Hayden came into the living room, still wearing her apron, beaming as she greeted Blake and Demi.

"You're much bigger than the last time I ran into you and your father," Grandma Hayden said to Demi with a smile. "What year are you in school now?"

Demi seemed a little shy. "I'm a freshman."

"I hear you like to barrel race and love rodeo just as my little Catharine did," Grandma said as she ushered everyone into the kitchen.

Demi nodded. "I love it."

The kitchen had always been the gathering place for family and friends. It smelled of melted cheese and pasta, a smell that had always been comforting to Cat.

Blake smiled and had a lively discussion with Grandma Hayden and she looked as pleased as could be. Demi and Cat talked about horses and the upcoming rodeo. Demi was excited and her enthusiasm was barely contained. When they talked about her favorite subjects, she seemed to forget about resenting Cat.

Even though Blake was engaged in conversation and wore a smile while talking, there was something in his eyes that told Cat he was troubled.

After dinner, Demi volunteered to wash dishes and they all cleaned up.

"We'll have dessert once dinner has had a chance to settle," Grandma said. "Would you like to play a card game?" she asked Demi.

The girl nodded. "Where are your cards?"

"Blake and I are going to go out on the porch for a few moments." Cat smiled at her grandmother. "We'll be back in a few."

"You go right ahead." Grandma was showing Demi where the decks of cards were. "We'll get the cards warmed up."

Blake walked with Cat onto the front porch and they closed the screen door behind themselves. It was a pleasant evening, the air cool and smelling of cut grass from the neighbor's yard. They sat in the porch swing like they'd done so many times when they were teenagers.

He looked like he was brooding over something, his gaze focused on a cottonwood in the front yard.

"What's wrong?" Cat finally asked.

For a long moment Blake didn't answer. Then he reached into his back pocket and pulled out papers that had been folded enough times to fit into his pocket.

She unfolded the papers and held them up so that the light from the living room window would allow her to read it. Her skin prickled as she read the start of the papers.

"It's a court order for a paternity test." She looked at the next set of papers. "And an order for Demi to be tested, too." Her eyes were wide as she looked at Blake. "Is that to prove you're Demi's father?"

He rubbed his temples with his fingertips then lowered his hand. "Sally called today. She claims that Demi isn't mine. Said she only married me because I have money and the biological father didn't."

Stunned didn't begin to describe the way Cat felt. She couldn't imagine what Blake was feeling right now.

"She wants to take Demi away from me and file for full custody." His voice was hoarse, like his emotions were almost too difficult to contain. "She's moving to Nashville. She'll take Demi halfway across the country from me if she wins custody."

"Dear God, Blake." Cat took his hand in hers. "What are you going to do?"

"I'm going to fight for her with everything I have." Blake's expression had darkened. "I don't give a shit what any test might say. Demi is my daughter and Sally isn't going to rip her away from me."

Cat couldn't think of a word to say. She squeezed his hand, trying to give him what comfort she could.

"Damn." He rubbed his eyes with his thumb and forefinger. "I'll call my lawyer Monday morning and do whatever I have to do to keep my daughter."

"Have you told Demi yet?" Cat asked.

He shook his head. "I need to get the blood tests done first to make sure this isn't one of Sally's games."

Blake gripped Cat's hand tightly and she rested her head on his shoulder. For a long moment they remained silent, the swing swaying a little with their slight movements.

"We'd better get inside," Blake finally said. "I don't want to keep your granny waiting."

Cat got up with him and as he released her hand, she wrapped her arms around him and hugged him for a long moment.

"I'm here for you, Blake," she whispered.

He put his forehead against hers. "Thank you."

When they drew away, he rested his on her lower back as they moved to the screen door and into the house.

Demi and Grandma Hayden were laughing as they played some kind of card game at the kitchen table. Blake put on a smile and pulled up a chair next to Demi and Cat sat between him and Grandma.

Cat watched Blake as he teamed up with Demi to play nertz, a card game, against Grandma Hayden and Cat. She watched the loving way he played the game with his daughter and how he always included her in the adults' conversations. In turn, it was clear how much Demi loved her father.

Cat's gut was sick and she prayed that Blake wasn't going to lose custody of his daughter. It would break his heart.

CHAPTER 18

"Why do I have to have a physical?" Demi asked Blake as they sat in the doctor's office. It was a week after Sally's call, the first opening they'd had at the doctor's office. "I'm not sick."

"Teenagers should have physicals done to make sure everything is all right, honey." He smiled at her. "But I hear they're not real fun for women."

"What do you mean?" she asked.

He felt heat rising to his face. "Dr. Mack will explain everything." He dug in his pocket and handed Demi her cell phone. "It's been a week now."

"Thanks, Dad." She took the phone, turned it on, and relaxed in one of the chairs as she started checking text and phone messages.

Blake had no idea if the boy, Brett, had sent her messages. He didn't want to violate his daughter's trust. But if she violated his trust again, then he would consider screening her messages.

Demi's name was called and they both got to their feet and she pocketed her cell phone. He accompanied her as a nurse took Demi's temperature and blood pressure as well as weighed her and measured her height. Then they went into the examination room where they waited for the doctor.

Blake and Demi talked about the upcoming rodeo while they waited, and he felt more and more uncomfortable.

When Dr. Mack and a fairly young nurse walked in, Blake wasn't sure if he felt relief or more tension than he'd been feeling before. Dr. Mack was in his early sixties, a good guy whom Blake had always liked.

"Honey, will you be okay if Dr. Mack talks with you alone?" Blake asked. "Now that you're a teenager you can have conversations with the doctor without me around."

Demi nodded. "Okay."

Relieved, Blake left the examination room and went to the waiting area. He forced himself to sit down rather than pace.

This was a time when it would have been good for Demi to have a woman in her life. Someone stable who could explain things like women's physicals so that his daughter would be better prepared.

He'd thought about Sally going with Demi to the doctor, but Sally hated that kind of thing and he was the parent with full custody. Not to mention, he needed to be with Demi when the blood tests were done and he didn't want Sally spilling the reason why they were having them done in the first place. He didn't want her to go through the pain of thinking about him possibly not being her biological father if it was unnecessary.

He wished he could have had Cat along. But even though Demi wasn't sulking as much, he didn't think she was ready for she and Cat to be doing things so personal together.

His lawyer had said there was precedent in Arizona where adoptive parents were given joint custody, so it was likely Sally couldn't win full custody. However, it was possible that Blake could get only partial custody and end up only having her on some holidays and during the summer. Sally would take Demi away to Tennessee. As far away as that was, it might as well be in another country.

He rubbed his temples. Damn. He couldn't lose Demi like that. He couldn't stand not being able to see her every day.

When Demi came out into the waiting room, Blake's tension rose. His daughter looked okay, but somehow seemed more adult as she walked outside with him.

"I didn't like that," she said, then handed him a paper. "The doctor told me that I also have to have some blood tests done."

Blake nodded. It was what he'd expected. At the same time they would have blood drawn for the court-ordered tests as well.

He drove them to the lab next and they both had their blood drawn. Demi refused to look at the needle as it pricked her skin and her jaw was set as she clenched her teeth. She'd always hated shots when she was younger, like most kids did, and having her blood drawn was no better as far as she was concerned.

She frowned as they walked outside the lab building. "I didn't like having my blood drawn."

He put his arm around her shoulders. "You did great."

"Why does the doctor need to do blood tests?" she asked as they reached the truck.

Blake opened the truck. "They just need to make sure everything is okay. Kids can get sick from things that need to be treated."

After they climbed in, Demi said, "Like Cat's daughter? She got sick so young."

He started the vehicle. He and Cat had talked about her daughter and she'd shared about what had happened to her. "Yes, they look for things like that." He gave Demi a comforting smile. "But thank God those things are rare."

She nodded and looked at him. "I love you, Dad."

Love and pain filled his heart and it was almost too much to bear. "Just remember how much I will always love you, too. No matter what."

* * * * *

Demi's cell phone rang and Blake watched as she pulled it out of her pocket and looked at the display. She flopped in a kitchen chair and answered, "Hi, Mom."

His shoulders always tensed when Demi talked to her mother and he mentally shook his head. He went back to pouring a glass of iced tea and squeezed lemon into it.

"I'm doing good." Demi had a light note to her voice as Blake wiped lemon juice from his fingers on a hand towel. "I missed sixth hour at school today which was okay with me. I hate math." She listened then said, "I didn't go because Dad and I went to the doctor today. I had to have a physical. It sucked."

A pause and then Demi frowned. "How did you know I had

blood tests done?"

Blake's gut clenched. When he'd talked with Sally earlier this week he'd asked her not to say anything to Demi until the results were back and to let him tell her.

Blood drained from Demi's face and she turned pale as she listened to her mother. Her eyes were wide as she looked at Blake. Then she said in a choked voice. "Dad isn't my real father?"

Blake felt like his heart had stopped beating. Confusion and pain clouded his daughter's face. He didn't know what to do as Demi stared at him as if begging him to challenge what her mother had told her. What could he say? He didn't know for sure.

She sat frozen with the phone held up to her ear. She didn't move when Blake took the phone from her and disconnected the call without saying anything to Sally. He turned the phone off so that she couldn't call back and disturb them.

As his daughter stared, he crouched in front of her chair and met her gaze. "Honey, your mother told me a week ago that I might not be your biological father." He put his hands on her shoulders. "But I don't care what any damned tests say. I *am* your father. I love you more than anything in this world."

"That's why my blood was taken today?" she whispered. "To prove that you're not my real dad?"

"I am your real dad." Blake's fury at Sally was hard to contain as he tried to reassure Demi. "No matter what, I love you and you are my daughter."

"Then why did you make me take the blood tests?" She looked as if she'd been betrayed.

"Your mother got a court order for both of us." He tried to keep his voice calm. "I had no choice."

Demi's lower lip trembled and tears started rolling down her cheeks. She shoved her chair back, got to her feet, and bolted out of the kitchen.

"Demi!" Blake went after her, heading for the front door.

She was ahead of him, running as fast as she could for the barn.

He followed her. Just as he reached the barn, Dandy tore out with Demi riding her bareback, her face streaked with tears.

"No, Demi," he shouted. "You know you're not allowed to ride bareback. It's too dangerous."

But she didn't heed him and probably couldn't hear him, as fast as she was riding.

"Damn." Blake ran into the barn and brought out Tango, his fastest mare. He threw a saddle on the horse and cinched it securely before he mounted and went after Demi.

She was nowhere in sight. The pain inside him for what Sally had just done to Demi mixed with fear for his daughter. She shouldn't be riding bareback, especially not in the emotional state she was in.

He headed Tango in the direction Demi had gone, the horse's hooves flying over the ground. They went over a small hill. Just as they crested it, he saw Demi's horse in the distance. The horse was riderless. As he got closer he saw a still form on the ground beside Dandy.

Blake's heart thundered and his entire body felt like ice. The fear in him was so great he felt like a knife had slashed his gut. What if what had happened to Cat had happened to his daughter?

When he reached Demi, her horse was nudging her as if to wake her up, but Demi didn't move.

He dismounted in a rush and went to Demi's side. She was so damned still. He placed his trembling fingers at her neck and found that her pulse was beating strong and sure.

Demi blinked and looked at Blake from where she lay on the ground, her expression confused. "What happened?"

"You took a spill off of Dandy." Blake stroked her hair. "Does anything hurt? Can you move your legs and arms?"

She shifted and pushed herself to a sitting position and rubbed the back of her head. "I have a lump but I think I'm okay." She frowned. "My hair feels sticky."

Blake looked at the ground and saw that a rock was where Demi's head had been and it was covered in blood. The fear that had never left him rose into his throat and he gently examined the back of her head. Her blonde hair was dark and matted with blood.

"Ow." She flinched.

"Don't move." He had to work to control his voice as he pulled a bandana out of his back pocket. He folded it and wrapped it around her head. "I'm going to get you to the ER."

"I'm okay." She winced as she spoke. "I just hurt my head, that's all."

"You were knocked out so you probably have a concussion," he said. "The doctors need to make sure there's no other damage or fractures." He stood with her as she got to her feet. "Do you think you can ride?"

She swayed a little and favored one leg as she grasped Tango's saddle. "I'll be okay," she said after a moment.

He helped her mount Tango and she gripped the pommel. He walked between the two horses, holding Tango by the bridle and resting his hand on Dandy's neck. As they headed toward the ranch, he kept a close eye on Demi to make sure she wasn't going to fall.

While they walked, Demi was silent. She looked like a heavy weight was on her mind. She looked down at him. "Mom said you might not be my father."

"I am your father, honey," Blake said.

She was silent again.

When they got to the barn, he helped Demi dismount then quickly unsaddled Tango and put both horses in their stalls.

Demi limped a little as they started walking. "Ouch," she mumbled and Blake's stomach twisted.

The drive to the hospital took too damned long as far as he was concerned. Once they were in the ER, while the nurse started taking Demi's vitals, Blake stepped away and called Sally.

"We need to talk," he said when Sally answered. "That was no way to tell a girl that her father might not be hers, even if it might be true. You had no right to do that."

"I can tell her any damned way I please," Sally said.

"Well, thanks to that stunt, Demi got upset and took off bareback on her horse." He clenched his jaw. "She fell off the horse."

Sally's voice grew shrill. "Is she all right?"

"She probably has a concussion and she might have broken something," Blake said. "Other than that, she's fine."

"I'm on my way," Sally said. "A girl should have her mother."

She should have considered that years ago, Blake thought as Sally disconnected the call.

After talking with his ex-wife, Blake talked with Cat to fill her in. She'd been upset and had offered to come to the ER to be with them, but with Sally coming it probably wouldn't be a good idea.

Because Sally currently lived in an apartment in town, she arrived within fifteen minutes.

"Are you all right, baby?" Sally rushed to Demi's bedside when the nurses directed her to Demi's room. She looked the girl over. "Where are you hurt?"

Blake said nothing, just folded his arms and watched as Sally made a fuss over Demi. He wondered how much of it was real and how much was for show. He dragged his hand down his face. Maybe he wasn't being fair. Sally genuinely cared for Demi, at least in her own selfish way.

"I'm okay," Demi was saying. "I just have a headache and my right leg hurts a little."

Sally whirled on Blake. "This is your fault. If she were with me this never would have happened."

Blake didn't repeat that what had happened to Demi wouldn't have if it hadn't been for the way she'd broken the news to Demi. It wouldn't help anything right now.

Sally turned back to Demi. "You're going to come live with me soon."

Demi's brows furrowed and she looked at Blake.

Before Sally could say anything else and before Demi could answer, he took Sally by the arm and led her out to the hall outside of the room.

"At least wait until Demi's out of the hospital before you start fighting over her," he said in a tight, low and angry tone. "She doesn't need this right now." Sally started to speak but he raised his finger. "As a matter of fact, don't fight in front of her at all. We'll work this out without turning her against either one of us."

"You have no say." Sally glared at him. "You're not her real father."

"I am her father," he said. "I've raised her as my own for fourteen years and my name is on the birth certificate."

"It won't be for long," she said in a cold voice.

The fury burning inside Blake threatened to burst out of his control. He fought down his anger.

"If you upset her while she's in the hospital it's only going to make things harder on her." He took a deep breath. "Let's make a truce while we're around her. No talking about who is and who isn't her father and no talking about ripping her away from her home. There's time enough to discuss any of that later."

Sally glared at him then faced Demi's hospital room. He saw her plaster a fake smile on her face before she strode through the doorway to Demi's side. He followed her and stood back as he watched Sally sit beside the bed and start talking with their daughter.

After the CAT scan and x-rays, the doctor gave his diagnosis. Demi did have a concussion and a fracture in her right leg. She was going to be in a cast for six weeks.

"No." Demi shook her head and pushed herself up in the bed when the doctor mentioned the cast. "The first rodeo of the season is this coming Saturday. I can't compete with a cast."

"You're not going to be riding for a while, I'm afraid," the doctor said.

"No," Demi repeated, looking horrified. Her gaze went to Blake. "Dad, don't let them put a cast on me."

The concussion was obviously making it difficult for Demi to absorb the news and realize that Blake couldn't just tell the doctor to not put a cast on her.

"I'm sorry, honey." Blake went to her side and took her hand. "It will only be for six weeks. You can compete after that."

He wasn't sure whether he was making a promise he couldn't keep. If Sally was awarded custody and took Demi to Tennessee, would she let her continue to work with horses, stay in 4-H, and compete in rodeos?

Tears rolled down Demi's cheeks and he felt her pain as if it were his own.

CHAPTER 19

Blake's gut churned as he walked from the mailbox at the end of the driveway, back to the house, carrying an envelope. It had been nearly two weeks since the paternity test and Demi's other blood tests, and there was no doubt in his mind what was in that envelope.

He didn't want to open it, afraid of what the papers would say.

When he reached the house, he sat on the top porch step. He pulled out his pocketknife and slit the envelope open before closing the knife and sliding it back into his pocket.

Cat came out of the house and quietly sat beside him. Demi wasn't home from school yet and Cat had come over to help him get together some records that the IRS auditor had requested.

He opened the paper, saw the results, and closed his eyes. It was there in black and white. Demi wasn't his biological daughter. He hung his head as Cat took the papers from him.

In his heart, Demi was his. But this would make it easier for Sally to try and take his daughter away from him.

"I'm so sorry," Cat whispered and put her head on his shoulder and held his arm, offering him comfort and he leaned into her.

He'd known this was coming. As sure as Sally had sounded and from her statement that she'd known she was pregnant before she met him. Also, the callous way she had chosen him to be the father of another man's child was something he could easily believe.

But Blake had to thank God that Sally had picked him out to be Demi's father or he would never have had her in his life. He was beyond angry that Sally could have the opportunity to take Demi away.

"Demi is mine," Blake said, for a moment not realizing he'd said it out loud.

Cat nodded, her head sliding over his arm. "In every single way that's important, she is your daughter." She raised her head and handed him the papers.

He got to his feet as he saw the bus in the distance, coming down the road. He folded the paternity test results and put them into his back pocket.

Cat stood. "I'll be in the house."

It was the Friday before the last week of school and then summer vacation started. He walked to the end of the driveway and waited for the bus, like he had every day since Demi had fractured her leg.

When the bus pulled up, Blake went to the door and greeted the bus driver.

Demi stood and handed him her crutches. "Hi, Dad."

He took the crutches along with her backpack. "Hi, honey."

She used the railing to climb down the stairs. He helped her situate herself with the crutches and then they started down the driveway toward the house. She was moving around well with the crutches these days.

"You got the letter today, didn't you," Demi said, stating it as if she knew it was fact.

"You can read me pretty well." Blake nodded. "Yeah, got it a little bit ago."

She looked at the ground as they moved. "It's not good news." Again, a statement.

"Does it make you feel any different about me being your father?" he asked.

She met his gaze and frowned. "No."

"That's how I feel." He put his hand on her shoulder. "You are my daughter. You will always be my daughter. Nothing has changed. Nothing. It's only a piece of paper."

She nodded as she reached out and gave him the tightest hug he had ever felt from her. "Agreed."

He thought about how Sally had broken the news and anger rose up inside of him. The anger wouldn't help. Even though Demi had found out in a really bad way, she'd become accustomed to the fact that there was a good chance he wasn't her bio dad and had handled that fact well just now.

"Cat's here," Demi said as she gave a nod toward Cat's truck. "Isn't she usually at work this time of day?"

"We had some accounting to take care of." Blake pushed his free hand through his hair. "I'll be glad when this audit is finished."

They reached the house and he helped Demi up the stairs and in through the front doorway and then headed into the kitchen.

"Hi, Cat." Demi made her way to a chair at the kitchen table, hopped as her dad took her crutches, then sat.

"How's your leg feeling today, Demi?" Cat brought a pitcher of lemonade out of the fridge.

Demi put her elbow on the table, her chin in her hand. "My leg is okay. I want to ride so badly. I guess I know how you felt when you couldn't ride for three years."

"Only four more weeks." Cat reached into the cabinet for some glasses. "Want some lemonade, you two?"

"I'd love some," Demi said.

"Sounds good." Blake reached into the pantry. "So do Oreos."

Demi and Cat agreed.

"Can Amy come over tonight?" Demi asked. "It's not a school night."

"Sure." Blake nodded.

"Cool." Demi pulled her phone out of her jeans pocket and called her friend. Usually Blake didn't allow her to make calls at the table but he was a little more lax about that now that she couldn't get around as easily.

After their afternoon snack, Demi braced her palms on the table and pushed herself to her feet. "I'm going to my room." She hopped to her crutches that were up against the wall. "I want to surf the 'net before Amy gets here."

Blake grabbed her backpack and carried it as he followed her down the hall. When they reached her room, she put her crutches nearby and sat at the writing desk where she kept her laptop most of the time.

He set her backpack beside the desk. "Will you and Amy be okay here while Cat and I go out? There's leftover pizza in the fridge."

"I'm getting around pretty good now and I'll have Amy to help." She nodded. "Where are you going?"

"To the Italian restaurant downtown," he said. "I'll bring home an order of ziti to heat up for tomorrow."

Demi smiled. "Yum."

He tugged on her braid. "See you later, kiddo."

"Daaaaad," she said.

"I know." He grinned. "Don't call you that."

CHAPTER 20

"Why don't we eat in tonight?" Cat tilted her head to meet Blake's eyes as he opened the front door to her home. "We can pick up dinner and have it here."

"Good idea." He let them into her house and closed the door behind them.

The house was quiet save for the sound of Sam running in his wheel. Her home still smelled of spring flowers from the scented candle she'd burned last night.

She called in an order to the Italian restaurant downtown, including an extra order of ziti to put in the fridge for Blake to take to Demi when he headed home.

While he was picking up the order, Cat opened windows and let in the sweet-smelling evening spring air. It smelled of the neighbor's fresh-cut grass and the roses beneath her windowsill. She turned on the stereo and soft music played as she lit several candles.

She looked at Sam's habitat and saw sparkly things in his nest. The little monster had escaped again and stuffed his cheeks with goodies, and had returned before she got in. He looked at her disapprovingly as she opened the lid to the habitat and picked out an earring back and two sparkly black sequins that must have fallen off of an evening dress in her closet, along with a white pearl sweater button she'd been missing for some time now. She'd wondered if it would turn up.

After Blake returned, they ate at the kitchen table. She served the Italian takeout on china plates and he lit a slender candle at the center of the table. She'd brought out a bottle of Merlot and two crystal wine stems and they drank the entire bottle while eating ziti, garlic bread, and a tossed salad she had put together while he was gone. They had also ordered tiramisu to eat later.

Blake smiled as they talked, but there was something in his eyes that told of the sadness and concern in his heart. She felt his pain as if it were her own.

When they were finished eating and everything was cleaned up, she told him, "You need a massage." She took him by the hand and led him to her bedroom where she turned on a small bedside lamp. "Strip so that I can take care of you."

"You just want to get me naked," he said with a grin.

"There's that, too." She smiled and watched as he tugged his T-shirt over his head, toed off his boots, and took off his jeans and boxer briefs.

He was such a magnificent specimen of a man, every muscle

well defined, not to mention being extremely well endowed.

She pointed toward the bed and good-naturedly he laid facedown on the comforter, his head to the side as he watched her. His eyes glittered in the low lighting as she slid out of her own clothing so that she was naked, too, and climbed onto the bed then straddled him.

"I don't know how long I can keep my hands off you," he murmured.

"Shush." She moved her hands to his upper arms. "You'll do as I say."

He gave a low laugh. "Yes, ma'am."

Muscles in his shoulders were knotted when she felt them with her fingers. Slowly, she worked out the knots. He gave groans of pleasure as she massaged his neck and his scalp before moving down to his back.

The tension in his body started to ease as she gave him a deep massage. His face was still turned to the side, his eyes closed, as he clearly enjoyed the magic of her fingers. She made her way from his upper to his lower back and then on to the tight globes of his ass as she massaged his muscular glutes and thighs.

"Damn," he murmured. "You're even better at this now than you were then."

She smiled. "I took a course in massage therapy several years ago. It's nice to be able to put it to good use."

"You can put it to use on me anytime, honey," he said and then groaned as she moved down to his calves.

He'd been so tense everywhere, but as she knelt between his thighs and massaged his feet, she sensed the nearly complete relaxation he felt now.

She eased back up his body so that she was straddling his waist. She grasped his shoulders, lowered her head, and nuzzled the curve of his neck, drinking in his masculine scent.

"Why don't I give you a massage now?" he murmured, sounding completely decompressed.

"This time is for you." She kissed his ear. "Next time you can take care of me. Now roll over. I'm not finished."

When she moved to the side, he rolled over and then she straddled him again. His cock was fiercely hard.

"I want you now," he said, his jaw tense.

"Hold yourself back, big boy." She massaged his temples and his face muscles, kissing him here and there as she moved her fingers. "Isn't that better?" she asked him as she rose up to look down at him and he grunted.

She worked her way downward, kissing him, touching him. He tensed again, but in a whole different way.

As she eased down, she kissed his erection, flicking her tongue over the head and tasting the semen at the tip. She moved her mouth along its length and he groaned.

"You've always known how to drive me crazy." He slipped his fingers into her long black hair, running them through the strands that slid over his abs in a silken wave.

"I do my best." She lightly bit at the inside of his thigh as she cupped his balls in her hand. She nipped the opposite thigh before she moved up his body again and grasped his cock in her hand. With her eyes focused on his, she squeezed his balls and slid him into her mouth.

"Damn." He let out a hiss of air as she tasted him, licked him, sucked him. "I don't know if you could drive me much crazier."

"I'm trying," she said before she moved her head down again, taking him deep before rising back up again, her hand moving with the motion of her mouth. She wanted to close her eyes and fall into the sensation of taking him in, but she knew he liked it when she watched him.

His body seemed to go rigid and then he was grasping her by her upper arms and drawing her up so that she was straddling his hips, his erection against her folds. She looked down to see him pressed against her.

"You're so beautiful." He pushed her hair out of her face. "Look at me. I want to see your eyes."

Smiling down at him, she rose up on her knees and grasped his cock. They watched each other as she put it at the entrance of her core.

It didn't look like he was even breathing as she started to slide downward along his length. He gritted his teeth as if holding himself back from taking her fast and hard, and her eyes widened as he filled her. She didn't know if she'd ever get used to how big he was.

She began riding him and he grasped her slim hips as she moved up and down.

"That's it." He moved his hands to her breasts and began pinching and pulling her nipples, causing her to gasp with pleasure.

"Blake." She was barely able to say his name. She was hardly able to breathe, much less talk.

He thrust his hips up higher, an explosive sensation traveling through her, warming her body, the heat causing a sheen of perspiration to cover her skin. He pinched her nipples more firmly as they moved together and she squirmed with the need to climax.

She rode him harder and lowered herself to give him a fierce kiss. He slipped his fingers into her hair, cupping the back of her head, and gave her an equally intense kiss.

As she rose back up, her hair fell down her naked back, sliding across her skin. She felt her orgasm coming closer and increased her pace. Her breathing came faster and she saw the rise and fall of his chest that showed he was breathing harder, too.

She could feel herself climbing up to the peak, coming closer and closer to orgasm. She saw in his face, too, that it wouldn't be long before he climaxed.

"Come on, sweetheart." He gave her a look of barely restrained wildness.

A gasp escaped her lips as she reached the brink and then she cried out when she tipped over the edge. Her core throbbed and her body vibrated with her orgasm.

He caught her off guard and she yelped with surprise when he flipped her over onto her back and began taking her in earnest. He thrust hard and fast, making her orgasm even more intense.

And then he shouted and came hard, his body jerking with the force of his climax. He thrust even harder a few more times and then stopped, pressing his groin tight to hers.

He studied her for a long moment before he lowered his head and gave her a soft kiss. He drew his cock out of her then rolled onto his side, her head tucked under his chin.

"I love you, Cat." He kissed the top of her head. "I've always loved you."

She snuggled closer to him, feeling as though she might never come down from the high of loving him. "I love you, too, Blake. With everything I have."

He cuddled her tighter as if he planned to never let her go. And that was perfectly fine with her.

CHAPTER 21

The courtroom was much smaller than Blake had expected. His body remained tight and coiled as he waited for the judge to come back out of his chambers with Demi. Both sides had pled their cases. He hated having Demi there and having to tell the judge which parent she preferred to live with, putting pressure on her. But Sally had brought that on and there had been nothing that Blake could do about it.

In Arizona, the minor child could not choose which parent he or she might prefer to live with. However, the judge would listen to the minor alone in chambers where there was no fear of influence by either parent. The minor child could then speak his or her feelings more easily.

Sally sat on the right side of the court with her lawyer. She wore fairly conservative clothing with simple stud earrings, instead of the extravagant jewelry she'd worn when he saw her last. She had made herself up to be soft and appealing, a mother just wanting custody of her daughter. She'd married earlier in the summer and had moved to what was, according to her, a very large home outside of Nashville. The courts had been backed up and they hadn't been able to get a hearing until now.

Her new husband sat on the bench behind her. Irwin Taylor was a computer engineer who had apparently hit it big with a startup software company that he'd sold for millions before the stock market crash.

Blake's own lawyer sat beside him. He'd been positive Blake would at least get joint custody. But the thought of not having Demi with him most of the time caused his gut to clench. He hoped to God he'd get her most of the year and her mother would get her during the summers.

The past months had passed by too quickly. It was the end of summer and school would be starting again, soon. Today would determine whether or not Demi would be staying or leaving soon.

A door opened from the side and Demi walked out with the judge. The bailiff ordered all to rise until the judge was seated.

Demi's face was pale and her eyes downcast as she returned to her seat behind both Blake and Sally. She glanced at Blake, as if appealing to him with her gaze. Sally tried to catch Demi's eye, but the girl refused to look at her mother.

The judge started speaking and everything seemed to be a blur together in Blake's mind.

Custody rights of the biological mother… Rights of the adoptive father… Consideration of the situation… What was in the best interest of the minor…

Blake's gut felt sicker and sicker as the judge spoke.

And when the judge delivered his decision it felt like a jail sentence.

Sally was to have custody of Demi during the school year in Tennessee. Blake would have custody during the summers and on some holidays.

"No!" Demi jumped out of her seat and ran for Blake as soon as the judge made the statement. "I'm not going with her!"

Blake took Demi in his arms and held her as she sobbed. The judge ordered Demi back to her seat and she was torn away from him while the judge finished rendering his decision.

The backs of Blake's eyes ached and his throat grew tighter and tighter as he listened. Nothing seemed to register after the judge stated who had custody and when. A schedule would be drawn up showing which holidays each parent had custody of Demi.

Sally grinned with triumph as the judge left the courtroom and then she was hugging her new husband and her lawyer and making cries of delight.

She turned to look at Demi but Demi ran back to Blake, ignoring her mother when Sally called to her.

Blake knew he had to be strong for Demi. But as he held her, he felt like he was going to fall into pieces and break down, too.

He managed to keep control of his emotions, but barely. When Demi drew away and he saw her tear-stained face, he nearly lost it.

"I don't want to live with Mom." Demi hiccuped another sob. "I told the judge that I want to live with you."

"Hey." He brushed hair out of her face. "We'll figure something out."

"No," Demi said. "I'm not going with her."

"What are you talking about, Demi?" Sally came up beside the girl, a broad smile on her face. "Of course you're coming with me. We're going to have so much fun together."

"I want to stay with Dad." Demi buried her face against her father's shirt. "I don't want to go with you." Her voice came out muffled as she spoke.

"Come on, Demi." Sally had an irritated look on her face that Demi couldn't see, but Sally's tone was sugary-sweet. "Give your mother a hug. We need to go get your things and get ready to go."

Demi sobbed even harder. Blake had to pry her away and stand her up straight. He held her by the shoulders.

"I need you to be brave, honey." He swallowed and cleared his throat. "The judge made his decision and we have to do what he says." He tried to give her a smile. "You'll probably like it in Tennessee. You'll have a new life and new friends."

Demi shook her head. "I want to stay here with you and Dandy and all of my friends. I want to be in rodeos and barrel race and be in 4-H and go to my school. I don't want my life to change."

"We'll see about a horse," Sally said from behind Demi, her voice sounding strained now. "I'm sure there are stables somewhere nearby where we can keep a horse. We have plenty of money, so we can buy you a better one than Dandy. And I'm certain they have 4-H clubs and rodeo. The schools where we live are supposed to be some of the best in the country."

Blake's heart ached as Demi turned and faced her mother. "No horse is better than Dandy. I don't care about any of that and I don't want to go."

"We're going." Impatience was now in Sally's tone. "No more

arguing. You're coming with me now and we're going to stop by Blake's house and get some of your things. The rest he can ship."

Demi looked at Blake with a pleading gaze. He met Sally's eyes, hateful eyes. "Let me take her back to the ranch and you can pick her up there. Give her time to say goodbye to everything she's lived with for the past fourteen years."

Sally glared over Demi's shoulder. "Fine. We'll come by early in the morning. Our flight leaves in the late afternoon." She turned her voice sugary once again as Demi faced her. "You've never been on a plane. This will be fun for you."

Demi whirled and ran down the aisle and out of the courtroom. Sally started after her but Blake put his hand on her arm. "I'll take her home and talk to her. You can have her tomorrow."

"You'd better not be poisoning her against me," Sally said and clenched her teeth.

"I would never do that to Demi." He gave Sally a hard look. "I want Demi to be happy wherever she lives."

"Well, call me in the morning when she's ready," Sally said. "We're staying at the Hassayampa Inn on Gurley Street."

With a nod he turned and headed out of the courtroom in search of his daughter.

He found her in the waiting area, sitting in a chair with her elbows on her knees, her face buried in her hands.

"Hey, kiddo." He wanted to make her smile, but she said nothing. "Let's go home. We're having your favorite supper and we'll make homemade ice cream."

She still said nothing.

"After supper you can take Dandy for a ride and I'll take Tango," he said.

She looked up at him and sniffled. "Okay." She got up from the chair and leaned into him as they walked out of the waiting room and headed home.

* * * * *

Cat waited at the ranch for Blake and Demi to get back from the custody hearing. She hadn't gone to the hearing herself because it would have been awkward with his ex-wife there, even if the woman was married to someone else now.

Blake had sent Cat a text message a little while ago that he and Demi were on their way home. It was likely he didn't want to go into detail about what had happened in court today in front of his daughter.

Cat's stomach felt queasy as she wondered how everything had gone.

The sound of a truck coming up the driveway caught Cat's attention. She waited in the kitchen, not sure what she should do. Demi knew Cat would be here at the ranch, but who knew what kind of condition or mood Demi would be in and if she would be receptive to Cat being around. No doubt today had been an emotional day, no matter which way it had gone.

The front door opened and closed and then Cat saw Demi walk by, down the hall, her head hanging. And then Blake walked into the kitchen, looking haggard and defeated as he met her gaze.

Cat went to him, tears rising to her eyes. He wrapped her in his embrace, holding her tightly like he didn't want to let go. She didn't know what to say, all she could do was give him what comfort she could offer.

He drew back and dragged his hand down his face before meeting her gaze again. "I get Demi during the summers and on some holidays." His voice sounded like his throat was almost closed off. "Her mother is taking her to Nashville for the rest of the time. She's taking Demi tomorrow."

Tears rolled down Cat's cheeks as she felt his immense pain straight to her heart. "I'm so sorry."

"I'm going to check on Demi." He pinched the bridge of his nose with his thumb and forefinger. "I told her I'd fix her favorite supper, tacos."

"I'll get them started," Cat said as she laid her hand on Blake's forearm. After she helped with supper she planned to leave to give Blake and Demi some time alone.

"Thanks." He gave her a quick kiss before he turned back out of the kitchen and headed down the hall.

Feeling sick to her stomach for Blake and Demi, Cat got out the beef and started simmering it in a pan before she got out the cheese, tomatoes, onions, lettuce, hot sauce, and salsa. Blake returned after a while and together they fixed supper.

Time had gone by quickly since Cat had met Demi at that first 4-H horse club meeting. During the past couple of months they'd become good friends and had gone riding together among other things. Cat had worked with Demi on her form and on recovering from her fractured leg, too.

Supper was ready just as Demi walked into the kitchen, her eyes red and puffy. She saw Cat, went straight to her and hugged her. More tears rose up inside Cat, and when Demi drew away Cat hurried to wipe them from her eyes.

"I'll miss you." Demi's voice sounded hoarse from crying. "I'm going to miss everything."

"I'm going to miss you, too." Cat gave her another hug. "Why don't we go ahead and eat supper and then I'll leave so you can be with your dad."

"You can stay," Demi said. "I don't mind."

Cat offered the girl a smile. "I think it will be good for you and your dad to have some time alone."

Demi nodded. "Okay."

They settled down to eat. Blake tried to keep things lively with talk about the ranch and Demi tried valiantly to smile and participate in the conversation.

When they finished eating, Demi left to put her boots on to ride. An idea had been developing in Cat's mind during dinner.

"Where is Sally staying?" she asked.

Blake seemed distracted. "The Hassayampa Inn."

She nodded. "You two go along and ride while the sun's still up and I'll take care of the dishes and then head home."

Demi walked into the kitchen. Cat gave the girl a last hug goodbye. "I'm going to miss you," she told Demi.

"I'll miss you, too." Demi clung to Cat for a moment before she stepped back. She looked like she was trying not to cry again.

"I'll see you when you come to visit your dad," she said.

Demi nodded. "Bye."

After Demi and Blake left to go riding, Cat couldn't stop the tears. She hurt for Blake and she hurt for Demi. A father and daughter who loved each other as much as Blake and Demi did should never be pulled apart.

CHAPTER 22

As she drove back to Prescott from the ranch, Cat spoke to a young man at the front desk of the Hassayampa Inn. "I'd like Sally Taylor's room."

"One moment, please," the desk agent said.

Cat waited as there was a click and then a ringing sound. A moment later a woman answered. "Hello?"

"Hi, Sally?" Cat swallowed. "This is Cat Hayden."

There was a pause before Sally said, "Blake's girlfriend? What do you want?"

Cat took a deep breath. "I'd like to meet you at the Starbucks on Montezuma."

"Why?" Sally asked, sounding a little suspicious, but curious, too.

"I just want to talk," Cat said. "I can be there in fifteen minutes if that works for you."

Another pause. "All right. But I don't have long."

"Thanks." Cat took a deep breath. "I'll see you there."

Her stomach churned as she drove the rest of the way into town and made her way to the Starbucks. After she parked and headed into the coffee shop, she looked around but didn't see Sally.

Cat picked a small table with two seats and sat in the chair facing the doorway. When she saw Sally walk in, she felt a little relief that the woman had come, mixed in with an additional burst of nervousness.

Sally wore tight jeans and an emerald green button up blouse open just enough to show her cleavage. She wore heavy gold earrings with a matching bracelet and necklace.

"Hi." Cat went for a smile as Sally sat at the table. "Thanks for coming."

The woman didn't smile but Cat didn't sense animosity from her, either.

"I only came because I'm curious what you would have to say to me." Sally leaned back in her seat and studied Cat. She became conscious of her scar and Sally's parting shot the first and only time Cat had seen the woman before now. "Did Blake send you?"

Cat shook her head. "I didn't tell him I was coming to talk with you." Cat stood. "What would you like to drink? I'm buying."

Sally shrugged one shoulder. "A grande vanilla latte. Iced."

"Be right back." Cat was almost afraid the woman would disappear before they had a chance to talk. She was glad no one was in line as she gave her order to the barista.

It wasn't too long before she was sitting at the table again and she set the cold clear plastic cup in front of Sally with her iced latte. Cat had gone for a cup of coffee with half and half and sugar.

Sally took a sip of her drink, settled in her chair, and crossed her legs at the knees. She folded her arms across her chest. "What was it that you want to talk about?"

Cat shifted in her seat. "First of all, I want to tell you how much I admire you. I hope you don't mind me being direct. I have had friends and family who have dealt with addiction. I know how hard it is to overcome and it can't be easy, all that you've been through."

Sally looked taken aback, as if she wasn't sure how to take what Cat had just said to her.

"I'm certain it took a lot to make it." Cat felt the heat of the coffee cup in one of her hands. "But you came out on top after what you've gone through."

Sally seemed to take a moment to consider what Cat had said. "What is the point of this?" Sally finally asked.

Cat leaned forward on the table, clasping her drink in both hands. "I have known that little girl for only three months, but I have grown to love her. I know you've won custody of Demi and you're planning on taking her to Tennessee with you."

With a raised eyebrow, Sally said, "So?"

"I think you're a mother who loves her daughter." Cat searched Sally's gaze, trying to connect with her in some way. "I also think you want what's best for Demi."

Sally narrowed her brows. "Of course I do."

"I'd like you to consider this." Cat studied Sally. "You're taking a girl who's on the verge of becoming a young woman, away from all that she's known and loved, including her father."

Sally's body language became tenser. "Is this all that you wanted?"

Cat gripped the cup tighter. "To do what's best for Demi, please consider what she wants –"

Sally's eye's flashed as she cut off Cat. "What's best for my daughter is for her to stay with her mother. I won custody of her and I'm going to keep her."

"And that might work out well—I'm not here to say it won't," Cat said. "My own daughter died when she was four." Cat swallowed. "So I don't know what it's like to have a teenager, but I know what I see. It would be hard for me, to be in your shoes. I wish I had a daughter to love, to hug, to see, and to consider what's best for her."

Cat continued, "I'm not telling you to change what you're doing. It's just that she loves her Dad and he's everything to her. I know there's a part of Demi who's positively affected by her mother, a woman who has overcome a lot and greatly desires to have her daughter to raise. Substance issues can make it look like you don't love your child, but I believe you do."

Sally looked like she was going to say something but didn't and Cat went on. "I would love nothing better than for you to reconnect with Demi so that she can have her mom again. That matters. I'm just asking you this because I care for that little girl and I know you do too. While she is with you, please consider whether or not you having custody of her is working and what's best for her. And please try not to be influenced by any anger you might hold against her dad."

Again, Sally was quiet. "I think you've said enough on this subject," she finally said.

"Think about it." Cat held back a sigh. "Please."

"My husband is waiting for me." Sally uncrossed her legs, pushed her chair back, and stood. "We have some things to take care of before we leave in the morning, but my daughter belongs with me. I am her mother."

"I understand." Cat got to her feet, too. "Thank you for meeting with me."

Sally looked at Cat for a long moment. "I'm sorry about the rude name I called you at Blake's," the woman said before she turned and left the café.

Surprised at Sally's apology, and disappointed that their conversation hadn't achieved what she'd hoped, Cat watched Sally leave before heading to the doorway herself.

Cat wasn't sure if she'd done the right thing, but she'd felt the need to at least try. Maybe something she'd said to Sally would someday make some kind of sense to the woman. Maybe.

CHAPTER 23

Blake removed his Stetson as he walked into Cat's home and pushed his hand through the short strands of his hair. He set his hat aside on the back of the couch and took Cat into his arms and kissed her.

He held on to her tightly as if making sure nothing would take her away from him, like his daughter had been.

When he stepped back, she looked up at him, wishing there was something she could do about the pain she knew he'd felt ever since Demi had been taken from him more than two months ago. He wasn't one to talk a whole lot about his feelings, but he'd shared a lot with her and it was clear how much he missed his daughter.

Blake's gaze traveled over Cat's face and he stroked her cheek. "I need to talk with you," he said, his eyes serious. "I don't know when or where is the best time."

Her skin prickled and a sense of foreboding came over her. She searched his gaze. "How about here, right now?"

He dragged his hand down his face and nodded. "Might as well."

She went to the couch and sat on the edge of it, her heart thudding. Something wasn't right. He looked so serious. What did he have to tell her? He couldn't be breaking up with her, could he?

He lowered himself to the couch, facing her. He took her hands in his and studied her as if trying to find the words he wanted to say.

"What is it?" She tried to keep her tone light even though she was suddenly crazy with worry.

"I can't be this far from my daughter." He held Cat's hands. "I can't take not being with her."

The prickles on her skin became more intense. "What are you saying?"

He was quiet for a long moment as he searched her gaze. "I'm selling the ranch and livestock, and I'm moving to Tennessee."

Shock made Cat almost dizzy for a moment. "You're leaving?"

"I want you to come with me." He released her hands and cupped her face in his palms. "I don't want to live without you again."

Her mind seemed to spin and her eyes started to burn. She grasped his wrists and brought his hands away from her face. "I can't leave, Blake." She fought back tears. "I came back to be with Grandma Hayden. She's sick and getting worse. I can't let her go through her illness alone. She has no one else."

He let his hands fall to his lap and he looked down at them.

When he met her gaze again, he saw her tear-filled eyes and brushed a tear from her cheek with his thumb.

"We can bring your granny with us, Cat." Blake looked at her with an earnest expression. "We'll get a house big enough that she can have a portion of the house to herself."

Cat had to let things process for a moment before she responded. Her mind just kept whirling at the thought of Blake selling the ranch, picking up everything, and moving to another state.

"Thank you for that." Cat swallowed. She continued, her throat feeling nearly closed off, "But I don't think she'll leave. She loves her home and she has memories from before Granddaddy died." Cat pushed her fingers through her hair. "She's always said she wants to live her final days in that house and doesn't want to go to a rest home or retirement community, or anywhere else." Cat had a hard time speaking as she tried to work everything through in her mind. "I think she's too ill to travel, too. It wouldn't be good for her. But I'll talk to her."

Blake rubbed his eyes with his thumb and forefinger and she wondered if he was going to cry, too. When he moved his hand away there seemed to be a slight redness to his eyes. "I don't want to leave you," he said. "And I can't live without Demi, either. You two mean everything to me."

Tears rolled down her face in earnest. "A little ironic, isn't it? When I wanted to leave when we were teenagers, you were married to the land. Now that you're planning to go, I'm tied here."

He drew her into his arms and held her, rocking her as he tucked her head under his chin, drawing her in close.

"I'm so selfish, Blake." She sobbed hard against his chest. "I don't want you to go. I don't want to live without you."

"I can't do it." His voice sounded strangled. "I just can't be this far from her."

Her shoulders shook as she cried. She wanted to beg him to stay, but she knew it wasn't right. She couldn't ask him to choose her over his daughter. But she wanted to…she just couldn't help it.

"What are we going to do?" She wiped tears from her eyes with the back of her hand. "Do we say goodbye now?"

"I don't know what to do." He studied her. "I'd hoped you would come with me. Now, I just don't know what in the hell to do about us."

"There's nothing to do about us." Cat got to her feet and turned away from him, trying to control her tears. "You have to do what you have to do. You need to go to Demi."

His boots thumped on the floor as he got up from the couch and then he was taking her by her upper arms and turning her around to face him. "Cat. Look at me."

She straightened and tried to control her breathing and her emotions as she met his gaze. "I'm not mad at you…I understand. You have to take care of your daughter and I have to take care of my grandmother. But I think I need some time alone now."

He looked at her a long moment, his voice soft as he spoke. "I love you."

She almost lost it then. "I'll see you later."

He studied her for a long moment, then gave a nod and turned away. He picked up his hat. When he opened the door, he looked at her one last time before closing the door behind him.

Everything crashed down on her and she started crying so hard she felt like she was going to fall to pieces. This was far worse than the last time they'd been separated.

She went to her room and curled up on her bed, her sobs wracking her body. The pain inside her was so great she knew nothing would ever heal it.

It wasn't his fault, she understood that. But it didn't make it hurt any less.

The one true love in her life had returned only for her to lose it all over again. She'd never love anyone else the way she loved Blake.

* * * * *

"Hi, honey," Blake said over the phone to Demi. "How are you doing?"

"I hate it here." She sounded close to tears as she said the same words she almost always said when he asked her how she was doing. "I want to go home."

It had only been two months, so he couldn't expect her to like it in her new home yet. He hadn't told her he was planning to move to Tennessee. He wanted to sell the ranch and take care of anything else that needed to be handled beforehand so that she wouldn't be disappointed if it took a while for him to get there.

"Just give it some time." He tried to speak in a soothing tone. "How's that horse your mom bought you?"

Demi had a shrug in her voice as she said, "Caprice is all right. She's not Dandy, though. She's supposed to be a good barrel racer, but she's just not as good and it just doesn't feel right."

"Are you able to get any practice in?" he asked.

"Mom and Irwin are busy a lot of the time and aren't around to take me to the stables." Demi sounded more than disappointed.

"Mom isn't home a whole lot."

Blake's jaw tensed. Sally had insisted on custody of Demi yet was hardly spending any time with their daughter. Every time he talked with Demi it was the same thing—she was usually home alone.

"Your mother must be busy." He tried to keep his tone even. He wasn't about to pitch his daughter against her mother.

"Yeah, busy with her husband." Demi paused. "I heard them talking about a trip to Europe this December. I don't know if they're planning on taking me or leaving me with Mrs. Buford."

Mrs. Buford was apparently in her sixties and was the housekeeper and cook. She watched over Demi when Sally and her husband weren't around. Which seemed to be a hell of a lot of the time.

Heat burned under Blake's collar. Demi shouldn't be left with a caregiver who wasn't one of her parents. He'd find a place fairly close to Sally's home so that Demi could spend time with him when her mother wasn't around.

He'd decided that since he was going to make a new start of it, he'd like to run his own stables and raise horses. He planned to take Dandy and Tango with him and that should make Demi happy.

"Do you like Mrs. Buford?" Blake asked.

"She's okay," Demi said. "She does make good cookies. My favorites are the snicker doodles."

"You're pretty good at baking cookies yourself. You'll have to get the recipe and make some for me next time you come home," he said.

"Home and cookies sound good to me," Demi said wistfully.

"Have you been making some friends?" he asked.

"A couple of girls from school have been nice and I met some kids at my first 4-H meeting here." He pictured her hugging her stuffed horse as she spoke. "How's Cat?" Demi asked.

"She's good." Just hearing her name made Blake heartsick. It had only been that morning that he'd broken the news to Cat that he planned to move to Nashville and she'd sent him away. She needed time to process it. He needed her by his side. "She misses you," he added.

"I miss her, too," Demi said. "Tell her I said so."

"I will, honey."

They talked a bit longer and she asked him about the horses and the ranch, her uncles, and Grandma and Grandpa McBride.

The homesickness in her voice made his chest hurt.

"You call me any time you need to talk," he said. "I don't care when or where, you call me."

"I will, Dad." A hint of a smile was finally in her voice. "I love you so much."

"I love you too, honey."

When they said goodbye, Blake disconnected the call and stared out his front window for a long time.

CHAPTER 24

The wind stirred restlessly as Blake rested one boot on the lower rail of the wood fence of the training ring and pictured Demi practicing for the next rodeo on Dandy. She'd missed most of the rodeos she'd worked so hard to compete in. She'd only been in a few between the time she had her cast taken off and her move. He hated that something she loved so much had been taken from her. She might get established in Tennessee, and he hoped so, but it wasn't going to be easy for her.

Damn, he missed his little girl. This place just wasn't the same. Nine weeks had passed since she'd moved and it was closing in on Thanksgiving.

It wouldn't be long now before he moved. He'd had a feeling someone in the family would buy the ranch, and his brother, Gage, had stepped up to the plate. He was also going to buy the livestock, excluding the horses. Blake was taking all of them with him.

One of the good things about selling the property to his brother was that Gage was in no rush to take over the place. That gave Blake time to take care of all that needed to be done, including what was necessary to make the move, like buying a new home and property to set up his new stables.

He still hadn't told Demi. He planned to fly out to Tennessee during Thanksgiving week to look for a new home and he'd tell his daughter in person. He'd already talked with Sally about splitting time with Demi over that weekend. She'd sounded strange on the phone, like she'd had something heavy on her mind, but she had agreed.

His thoughts turned to Cat and his chest hurt like it always did. He understood why she couldn't go with him, but that didn't make it any easier. More than a week had gone by since he'd told her he was moving. She'd stayed away from him and he couldn't blame her although he missed her fiercely.

The sound of a vehicle coming down the road caused him to turn. His heart thumped when he saw that it was Cat's truck. The windows were tinted and he didn't get a good look at her until she parked and a few moments later climbed out of the truck.

Emotions warred in him as he strode toward her. He saw her beautiful face and the set of her jaw, the determination in her gaze.

When their eyes met, she ran toward him. He stopped, waiting for her, wondering if something had happened.

She reached him and flung her arms around his neck and pressed her body close to his.

"Blake." She tilted her face to look at him. "I can't do this. I can't just say goodbye. It hurts too much."

He studied her, loving the feel of her in his arms, never wanting to let her go. "What are you saying, honey?"

"I'll wait for you." Her throat worked as she swallowed. "We can do this long distance until Demi graduates from high school. It's four years down the road, but I'll wait for you. Having some of you is better than none of you." Tears glistened in her eyes. "That is, if you're willing, too."

"Hell, yes." He pressed her close to him, breathing in her scent, reveling in the feel of her body against his. "I'll come back to see you at least every three to four weeks and we can talk on the phone every day if you want." He took her by the shoulders and held her away from him, studying her. "If you're sure that's what you want to do."

She nodded. "We were apart for so long. Another four years isn't going to be easy, but I love you too much to let you go."

He caught sight of her wrist. "You still have it."

She looked down at the gold bracelet connected at the top with a heart. The one he'd given her for her eighteenth birthday.

"Of course." She smiled.

"My little KitCat." He drew her in once again and she clung to him.

* * * * *

The time they spent together that afternoon had been fierce, passionate, neither one of them wanting to let go of the other. It was like they were making up for lost time and for days yet to come when they would be alone.

When Cat had to return to town to check in on her

grandmother, Blake was reluctant to let her go, but knew she needed to.

They walked outside, hand-in-hand. They reached her truck and he brought her into his arms and kissed her.

He put his forehead against hers. "You know how much I love you, don't you?"

"At least as much as I love you," she said with a smile.

His phone rang. He was going to ignore it, but she pulled away. "It might be Demi."

He drew the phone out of the leather holster at his belt and looked at the caller ID screen.

"It's Sally," he said.

"Take it." Cat looked up at him.

He pressed the connect button and raised the phone to his ear. "Hi, Sally."

"Blake, I need to talk to you." Sally was hesitant, which was unusual for her. It was much like the odd way she'd sounded the last time they'd spoken.

"All right," he said, feeling wary as he turned away from Cat and stared out into the clear blue sky. "What do you need to talk about?"

"So much has happened and I've been doing a lot of thinking over the past three months." She paused, took an audible breath, then said, "I haven't touched drugs but I started drinking again."

Cold washed over him. "You what?" he said even though he knew he'd heard her right.

"Drinking. About two months ago." She sounded nervous. "But I started going to AA meetings again and I've been sober again for almost three weeks."

He pinched the bridge of his nose with his thumb and forefinger, trying to control his anger. "Demi can't live in that kind of situation," he said. "I can't let that happen."

"I know." Sally truly sounded like she truly knew she was in the wrong. "I'm working with my sponsor and as I'm working through the twelve steps I've come to realize some things. I don't know that I can give Demi everything she needs."

His brow furrowed. "You need money?"

"That's certainly not a problem." She gave a laugh, but it wasn't one of humor because her voice turned serious again. "My sponsor helped me to see that I've been selfish, and frankly, a total bitch."

Blake didn't say anything as his mind tried to come up with a solution to the problem that Sally had been drinking again. Even if she was sober now, the fact that she'd slipped was a huge problem.

"I've thought a lot about what Cat said to me after we'd gone to court over Demi," Sally continued and Blake glanced as Cat, wondering when she'd had a chance to talk to Sally and what she'd said.

"And as I work through this twelve-step program," Sally went on, "I've come to the conclusion that I'm not cut out to be a full-time mother. I started turning to alcohol again because it's all been so stressful and I've felt inadequate. I want to be that girl's mother so badly, but I know where she wants to be and I know I can't replace you."

He frowned. He could hear the emotion in her voice and thought she might be crying, but he wasn't altogether sure what she was trying to tell him.

"Cat was right," Sally said in a rush. "It's in Demi's best interest to be with you full-time."

Stunned, Blake couldn't think of what to say. He felt frozen as he tried to grasp what she was telling him. Somehow it wasn't sinking in.

"She's not happy here, either, and I'm gone a lot with my husband," Sally added before he could say anything. "I thought maybe she'd get used to it here and make some friends and be happy. I thought I would spend more time with her while having her live with me, but it hasn't worked out that way."

"You're giving custody of Demi to me," he repeated slowly when it began to sink in. "Legal?"

"I want her for some of the holidays, but yes, full legal custody to you." Sally sounded like she was unsure. "You still want her, don't you?"

"God, yes." A sense of elation swept over Blake and the corners of his eyes stung. He was going to have his little girl again.

"I was thinking she should probably finish the school year out here." Sally had a note of relief in her voice, as if she had thought he might refuse. "There's only about a few weeks left."

"That's probably a good idea." He agreed with Sally even though he would have given anything to have Demi back on the first flight to Phoenix.

"In the meantime," Sally said, "I'll have my lawyer draw up the necessary legal paperwork."

He gripped the phone tighter. "Have you told Demi?"

"No," Sally said. "I wanted to talk with you first to make sure you wanted to take her."

He realized he was grinning now as he met Cat's gaze. She was looking at him with surprise combined with amazement and joy.

"When are you going to tell her?" he asked Sally.

"Tonight, after she gets back from the stables," Sally said.

He felt almost high from the elation filling him. "Have her call me afterward,"

"I will." Sally almost sounded like she was going to cry. "Thank you, Blake. I've come to realize that you're a much better dad than I'll ever be a mother. I have an awful lot of work to do on myself."

He sighed, not wanting to bring her down. "She loves you, Sally. You know that."

"I know." A bit of a smile touched her voice. "She's just happier with you, living the life she was raised in." And then she sounded sad again. "I'm sorry I put you both through this. It wasn't fair of me."

"I'd still like to come out Thanksgiving week if that's all right with you," he said. "I'll stay in a hotel and work something out with you to take her out for the holiday."

"That's fine," Sally said. "One last thing." She sounded serious again. "Tell Cat thank you."

He nodded. "I'll do that."

"I need to get to my AA meeting," she said. "I'll have Demi call you tonight." Then Sally disconnected the call.

He lowered the phone and closed his eyes before giving a broad grin. He opened his eyes and whooped loud enough to startle a flock of birds that had been resting on a nearby fence rail.

Cat closed the short distance between them and he caught her up so that her thighs were around his hips, her arms around his neck. Her eyes sparkled and she looked nearly as happy as he was. He swung her around, grinning, and she laughed.

"My little girl is coming home," he said and felt his eyes burn again. "She's coming home."

CHAPTER 25

Cat walked hand-in-hand with Blake from the stables in Montana, leaving the horses to be brushed down by the stable hands.

Blake squeezed her fingers as they walked by the lodge and in the direction of their cabin, and she looked up at him and returned his smile.

"This has been the best honeymoon." She leaned into his arm. "Cat Hayden McBride. Has a great ring to it."

"Yes, it does." He caught her by the chin and tilted her face up and kissed her. "I have the most beautiful wife."

"And I have the sexiest husband in the west." She grinned. "Heck, the sexiest husband alive."

He laughed and put his arm around her shoulders. She didn't

think she could ever get enough of being close to him. It was June, a little over a year after Cat had first run into Blake at the 4-H horse club meeting. School was out, and Demi was with her mother while Blake and Cat honeymooned.

"When you talked with Demi, she sounded like she's having fun with her mom," Cat said as they approached the cabin. "I think Sally has come a long way during the past seven months or so."

"She has." Blake gave a nod. "I feel a lot more comfortable now letting Demi stay with Sally for an extended period of time. Even though I still miss my daughter."

"I think she's really enjoying going to the horse races with her mother and stepfather." Cat swung hands with Blake. "Pretty cool that Sally's husband has friends who have racehorses and that he likes to go to the races."

"Demi certainly loved the Kentucky Derby," Blake said with a nod. "Gives her something in common with her mom now."

"She has rodeo with you and horse races with Sally." Cat smiled. "I guess she has the best of both worlds."

"Mrs. Belleview seems to think your granny is doing well these days." Blake squeezed Cat's hand.

She nodded. "Grandma Hayden is pretty amazing, the way she's pulled through it all. She's so tough, nothing can keep her down."

They reached the cabin and Blake opened the door. He caught Cat off guard as he swept her up in his arms and she giggled as they walked through the door and he kicked it shut behind him.

It was called a cabin but it was pretty amazing with its huge vaulted ceilings, skylights, hot tub, and so much more. They would have been happy to spend their honeymoon together in a bare one-room cabin, but this had been a fun place.

Still carrying her in his arms, he headed up the stairs to the huge loft with the massive bed beneath the skylights. When he reached the bed she squealed with laughter when he tossed her onto the middle of the mattress.

He grabbed something from his duffel bag that was in the closet and then he eased onto the bed. She saw what it was as he straddled her.

"Rope?" she said as she grinned up at him.

He grasped her wrists and pulled her arms over her head. "I promised you that I'd tie you up. I need to show you that you're mine."

She laughed as he tied her wrists to a wooden rail of the headboard. "I'm already yours."

"Just making sure that you know it." He unbuttoned her blouse as she squirmed beneath him. Full sunlight shone through the skylights and she looked up at his hard but handsome face.

When her blouse was unbuttoned, he pulled her red bra beneath her breasts and her nipples tightened. He brushed them with the back of his hand and she bit the inside of her lip and arched her back, wanting him to do more than just touch her.

"You want more?" He dipped his head and sucked on one of her nipples.

She moaned. "Lots. And lots."

With a low laugh he said, "That's what I have in mind for you."

He eased down her body until he reached the foot of the bed, then grasped one of her boots and tugged it off. He removed her other boot, then pulled off each of her socks.

"Now that I can have my way with you, what should I do?" he

murmured just before he tickled the bottoms of her feet.

She wriggled, giggling. "Noooo. Not that."

He grinned and tickled her more, causing her to laugh so hard she could barely breathe. She begged him to stop once again and he moved back up her body and braced his hands on either side of her as he looked down at her.

"Will you behave?" he said, still grinning.

She nodded vigorously as she tried to stop laughing. "I promise."

He reached for the button of her jeans and unbuttoned them before drawing down her zipper. That calmed her laughter as she met his gaze and saw the smoldering look in his eyes. He adjusted himself so that he could strip off her jeans.

When she was left in her red panties, he ran his finger along the waistband. "You know how I love it when you wear red."

She nodded. "I wear that color just for you."

He stripped off her panties and now all she wore was the open shirt with her bra beneath her bared breasts and her arms tied over her head. As he watched her with a look of intense hunger, he stood and shucked off his boots and his clothing.

Her mouth watered and her body ached for him as she studied his incredible form and his erect cock that was hard just for her.

He moved between her thighs and braced himself over her again. His expression grew more serious. "I love you, Mrs. McBride."

She thought she'd melt from the way he was looking at her. He untied her wrists and she looped her arms around his neck and smiled. "I love you, Mr. McBride."

He slid inside her then, causing her to gasp with pleasure.

Slowly he moved in and out and she rose up to meet his every thrust.

Feelings of love swirled with the sensations whirling within her body, so intense she could barely focus on his strong features.

"Come with me, KitCat," he said. "Now."

She cried out as she climaxed and he shouted and shuddered with his own pleasure.

When he could control his breathing, he wrapped her in his arms and adjusted her so that he was on his back, her head on his chest.

"We have a lot of time to make up for," he said as he held her.

She smiled. "We certainly do."

Also by Cheyenne McCray

From St. Martin's Press:

"Night Tracker" Series
Demons Not Included
No Werewolves Allowed
Vampires Not Invited
Zombies Sold Separately
Vampires Dead Ahead

"Magic" Series
Forbidden Magic
Seduced by Magic
Wicked Magic
Shadow Magic
Dark Magic

Single Title
Moving Target
Chosen Prey

Anthologies
No Rest for the Witches
Real Men Last All Night
Legally Hot
Chicks Kick Butt
Hotter than Hell
Mammoth Book of Paranormal Romances
Mammoth Book of Special Ops Romances

Excerpt... Branded for You

Cheyenne McCray

The afternoon was cooling off as it turned to dusk and then darkness descended on them. They each grabbed a light sweat jacket from the camper and slipped them on.

Ryan took a couple of steaks out of the cooler to cook over the fire. Megan sliced the potatoes and wrapped them in foil with butter and seasonings and put them in the coals first. Ryan buttered, salted, and peppered the corn on the cob and wrapped them in foil, too. When it was time, they placed the corn along the edge of the fire. Ryan had cored out the onion and put butter in the center and wrapped it in foil and put it in the coals, as well. The steaks went on last, when everything else was just about finished cooking.

When it was ready, they sat on the camping chairs in front of the fire and ate dinner.

"This is unbelievable," Megan said with a smile.

Firelight flickered on her pretty features, casting shadows in the darkness as they ate. He thought about what he'd said to her earlier.

"I might be falling for you, Meg."

He didn't regret his words. He'd dated a lot of women in the past but there'd just been something missing. Something intangible that he hadn't been able to name.

He'd never been a love 'em and leave 'em kind of guy, but some thought so. He just wasn't going to hang in there with someone if he knew she wasn't the right one.

He'd never felt the same way with anyone that he did with Megan.

Last night he'd taken her hard and rough, and the memory caused his groin to ache. Damn she'd been amazing. But she needed to know that he wanted more from her than a night of good, hard sex.

When they finished dinner and had cleaned up, he brought a blanket from the camper and handed it to her before he put out the fire. After he extinguished the fire, he lit a candle within a glass and metal hurricane lantern.

He took her by the hand. "I've got something I want to show you." Her hand was warm in his.

She smiled up at him, her smile causing something deep inside him to stir. He led her into the forest, candlelight from the hurricane lantern lighting the way. The candlelight was much gentler than a regular camping lantern and the shadows from it bounced from tree to tree.

"I saw a place somewhere over here," he murmured as they walked through the forest then came to a stop. "Here we go."

A small clearing lay on the other side of a fallen tree, a bed of leaves at the center of the clearing. They stepped over the tree and then he found a sturdy place to set the hurricane before taking the blanket from Megan and spreading it out on the leaves.

He slipped out of his jacket and set it on the fallen tree. "I'll keep you warm," he said as he held out his hand.

She looked up at him, slid off her sweat jacket, handed it to him and he set it on top of his own.

He sat on the blanket and beckoned to her. She eased onto her knees beside him and he cupped her face in his hands and lowered his head and kissed her.

Her kiss was sweet and his desire for her kicked into full gear. He wanted to take her hard again, right now. But more importantly, he wanted to show her that it wasn't only about rough sex with him. It was all about her.

When he drew away from the kiss, her lips were parted, hunger in her pretty green eyes.

"You're an incredible woman." He brushed his thumb over her lips, which trembled beneath his touch. "I've loved every minute of this weekend."

"So have I," she said, her voice just above a whisper. "I wish it didn't have to end."

"It doesn't." He nuzzled her hair that was silky now that it had dried. "When we return, we just pick right back up where we left off."

She smiled and he kissed her again. She felt so soft and warm in his arms. He slid his hand under her T-shirt, pleased she didn't have her bra on as he cupped her bare breast and rubbed his thumb over her nipple. He watched her expression as her lips parted and her eyes grew dark with need.

He drew the T-shirt over her head and set it on the fallen tree. Candlelight flickered, gently touching her bare shoulders and chest.

"You know how much I love your body and how beautiful I think you are," he murmured before stroking her nipples with the back of his hand.

He cupped her breasts, feeling their weight in his hands before he lowered his head and sucked a nipple.

She gasped and leaned back so that her hands were braced behind her on the blanket, her back arched so that he had better access to her breasts. He pressed them together and moved his mouth from one to the other, sucking one nipple before moving his mouth to the other one. Her nipples were large and hard and he loved sucking on them.

"I want you on your back, looking at me." He adjusted her so that she was lying on the blanket. Her eyes glittered in the light, desire on her features.

He was surprised at how she made him want to go slow with her, to be gentle and show her how much he cared. She stirred things inside him he'd never felt with another woman.

EXCERPT... LINGERIE AND LARIATS

Cheyenne McCray

When they'd finished dinner and washed up the dishes, she walked with him to the living room. They paused and stood in the center of the room as he studied her and she met his eyes. Her belly flip-flopped at his intense gaze. He looked her as if she was a treasure he wanted to protect.

But at the same time he looked at her like a man who wanted a woman. A look of passion and need was in his gaze that couldn't be disguised.

He reached up and ran strands of her long hair through his fingers. "I want to kiss you, Renee."

She bit the inside of her lip as her own need expanded inside her. She slid her hands up his chest to his shoulders and offered him a smile. "I want you to."

His warm breath feathered across her lips as he lowered his mouth to hers. The intensity of the moment was filled with a kind of fire that made her burn inside.

Her eyelids fluttered closed as he brought his mouth to hers, and it was like magic sparked between them when their lips met. She felt as if her mind was spinning and stars glittered behind her eyes. She fell into the kiss, her head whirling, her heart pounding.

His taste made her want more of him and she made sounds of need and pleasure. He deepened the kiss and she gave a soft moan.

She reveled in his embrace, the feel of his hard chest against her breasts and the warmth and comfort of his arms around her. She strained to somehow get closer to him, to become a part of him.

A deep, rumbling groan rose up in him and he kissed her hard before drawing away. He still held her in his embrace and she loved the feeling of security she experienced in his arms.

She opened her eyes and stared up at him, her lips moist from his kiss, her breathing a little fast.

He gently brushed hair from her cheek as he looked down at her, and his expression turned serious. "I've wanted to kiss you from the moment I first saw you at the Cameron's place, but I shouldn't have done that. I don't want to take advantage of you in a vulnerable state."

For a long moment she looked up at him, studying the sea green of his eyes. "When I was a young girl, living with the Camerons, I had the biggest crush on you."

The corner of his mouth quirked into a smile. "Is that so?" he said in a lazy drawl.

She returned his smile. "When you saved my life, you became my hero as well as my crush."

"I thought you were pretty cute." He slid his fingers into her hair and cupped the back of her head. "And you've grown up to be one hell of a beautiful woman."

She placed her hands on his chest, reached up on her toes, and kissed him. His lips were firm and he returned her kiss, his kiss as hungry as hers. Searching, longing, and filled with desire. She gripped his shirt in her hands as she pressed her body tight to his. She didn't think she could get enough of him.

Judging by the hard ridge she felt against her belly, she knew he was as affected as she was by the moment.

He drew away again and she felt his rapid heartbeat against her palm and his chest rose and fell with the increased pace of his breathing.

"It was a mistake to kiss you because it only makes me want more. A lot more." He slid his fingers through her long, glossy hair. "I want so much more of you than that. But it's too soon."

She closed her eyes, letting her breathing slow. When she opened them again she found him watching her. Her voice seemed a little shaky. "You're right, it's too soon. All of this with Jerry has been so emotional. I'm feeling everything right now... Hate and anger for him, and strong feelings for you. But I shouldn't take things so fast no matter how right it feels with you." She brushed her fingers along his shirt collar. "And Dan, it feels so right."

"It feels unbelievably right." He lowered his head and gave her a firm, hard kiss then stepped back. Her palms slid down his chest and then he took her hands in his. "How about watching a movie and getting our minds off of certain things?"

"That sounds like a good idea." Not that she thought she could get her mind off of wanting to experience more with Dan. She gestured to the front door. "Why don't we watch the storm first?"

He took her small hand in his big one and they went outside onto the covered porch and closed the front door behind them. Patches of warm yellow light spilled from the house onto the porch.

The sky was dark, the occasional crack of lighting illuminating the trees and outbuildings for seconds before everything went dark again. The air smelled fresh and clean as wind pressed her clothing against her body and her hair rose up off her shoulders. A gust of wind sent a mist of wetness onto the porch and she smiled at the feel of warm summer rain on her skin.

As they watched the storm, he squeezed her hand and looked down at her. She met his gaze and smiled. They stood on the porch a while longer and she watched bolts of lightning slicing the sky as thunder rolled across the valley.

Excerpt... Roses and Rodeo

Cheyenne McCray

"No thank you." Danica turned down yet another offer from a cowboy to buy her a drink.

After she declined, she dismissed the cowboy with a genuine smile. She moved away to search the room with her gaze for Kelsey. She held onto her beer bottle as she moved through the crowd.

The bar was packed with men and women in western attire and a country-western band had been playing familiar tunes all night. She liked that the slot machines were outside the bar and the constant ringing and cha-ching of machines wasn't competing with the good music.

She'd caught herself lightly tapping her boot since she'd come into the bar, but she hadn't been in the mood to dance. Usually she did, but tonight she had a headache that alcohol hadn't been able to kick. Thank goodness smoking had been banned from bars and restaurants in Las Vegas or her headache would have magnified.

Her gaze slid past Creed who had three women around him. Kelsey had called the women buckle bunnies, female groupies. From what she'd seen, the groupies tended to wear tight jeans and boots with skimpy tops and bright, flashy accessories like a belt with a big buckle that had lots of dazzle.

She moved her gaze away from the cowboy and groupies then spotted her petite friend who was leaning against Darryl, her hand on his chest, looking into the tall cowboy's eyes. It was a sweet, romantic picture the way he was looking at her. Danica hoped Kelsey wouldn't get her heart broken. She'd been through far too much and she deserved a good guy. Danica had met him earlier in the night when Kelsey had introduced them. He seemed okay, but she'd reserve judgment for later.

Her cell phone had vibrated in her pocket three separate times. She was sure they were messages from Barry, so she didn't bother to look.

From the corner of her eye, she found herself looking at Creed. This time a woman who looked upset was talking with him and the buckle bunnies were gone. He reached up and brushed something from beneath her eye with his thumb. He said something to her and she nodded, then turned and walked in Danica's direction. The woman bumped into Danica, nearly making her drop her beer bottle.

Danica took a step back and shook her head. She looked at Darryl and Kelsey again. They really did look like a cute couple. She glanced away from the pair to check her watch. It was still early but she really wasn't in the mood to party. Maybe she'd tell Kelsey about her headache and that she was going to head up to their suite in the casino resort hotel that was on the strip. She wouldn't mind a bath in the amazing jetted tub.

"Heading off so early?" The deep drawl caught her attention. She immediately loved the male voice and turned to find herself facing Creed McBride.

She raised her brows. "Who says I'm leaving?"

He gave a slow, sexy grin. "Honey, you've been trying to head out that door all night."

Her face warmed. "You've been watching me?"

"Ever since you walked into the room." He searched her gaze. "Just waiting for a chance to catch your attention. I don't think there's a cowboy in this place who hasn't offered to buy you a drink."

She studied his eyes. He had dark hair and nice eyes that were a gorgeous shade of green. "Who's to say I'm not going to send you packing?"

His gaze held hers. "I'm hoping my luck will hold out. I think this is the longest conversation you've had with any cowboy you've met tonight."

Amusement sparked in his eyes as he spoke. He had that same ease and confidence in his manner in person as she'd seen before he'd ridden that bull and even after his ride.

He was about as tall as her four brothers, around six-two, but a little younger—she'd guess about thirty-three. His white shirt and Wrangler jeans fit him oh-so-well, and his white western hat was tilted up enough that she could study his eyes. He was definitely hot in an alpha male, bad boy kinda way.

"I'm Creed McBride." He held out his hand.

"My name is Danica and you're right, I'm heading up to my room." She smiled as she took his hand. "Nice meeting you," she added but couldn't get herself to turn away. In fact she had a hard time getting herself to release his hand. His grip was firm and warm, his hand callused from hard work.

It was probably only seconds but it seemed as though it carried on longer before she finally drew back her hand.

"Pretty name." He looked like he wanted to touch her again to keep her from leaving but held himself back. She didn't know why she thought he did, but she could almost feel the brush of his fingers against her cheek even though he hadn't reached for her at all. He studied her and she felt warmth go through her at the intensity in her look. "I bet you're told all of the time what gorgeous blue eyes you have. Such a brilliant blue," he said.

"Is that a pick-up line?" She raised an eyebrow.

"You know it's not." He smiled. "It's an observation."

It was true that she got that all of the time. She and her four brothers had the same eye color and her aunt called them "Cameron blue".

"Are you sure you wouldn't like to two-step with me?" Creed gave a nod to the dance floor. "I haven't had a chance to dance all night."

She wanted to ask him why not when gorgeous women had surrounded him all night, or the other woman he'd been talking with, but she didn't want him to know that he'd captured her attention tonight, more than once. Fortunately, she didn't think he'd caught her at it.

Darryl came up to Creed's side and he put his arm around Creed's neck. "Do you know who you're talkin' to?" Darryl raised his beer bottle with his opposite hand. "You should be damned impressed. This is Creed McBride, two-time world bull riding champion."

Creed looked uncomfortable and Danica's lips twisted with amusement as she teased him. "I'm impressed by a lot of things, but riding an animal out to kill you isn't one of them. I'm more impressed by the person."

"Felt the heat on that one." A slight grin curved the corner of Creed's mouth, obviously knowing she was teasing, and he disengaged from Darryl. "Why don't you go find that cute little blonde you've been with all night?" he said to Darryl.

Darryl turned his gaze on Danica and slowly looked her up and down. Disgust flowed through her at the blatant way he was undressing her with his gaze. "What about this sexy thing?" He grinned. "Danica, right?"

"Yes." She folded her arms across her chest. "Best friend to Kelsey Richards. Where is she, by the way?"

Darryl jerked his thumb over his shoulder. "She's waiting for me by the bar."

Danica put her hands on her hips. "I think I might need to go have a talk with her."

"Just havin' a little fun." Darryl straightened. "I best be getting back to Kelsey."

Danica frowned, wondering if she *should* go have a talk with her friend. But then Danica wondered if maybe she was reading too much into the way he'd been looking at her.

Darryl touched the brim of his hat. "Ma'am," he said politely, his demeanor completely changed. Darryl slapped Creed on the shoulder then turned and headed toward the bar where Danica caught a glimpse of Kelsey.

"Come on." Creed indicated that dance floor with a nod. "Give this cowboy a dance."

The only indecision that warred within her was the thought of getting to know him better, maybe even liking him, when she'd already decided that she wouldn't want to date a bull rider. Not that dancing with him meant that he even wanted a relationship with her.

Against her better judgment, she found herself nodding. "All right."

He flashed a smile at her and took her by the hand. She set her beer bottle on a table as they passed by and then they were on the dance floor.

It was a lively two-step and they fell into the dance as if they'd been doing it together forever. She'd been country-western dancing since she was a little girl and it was obvious he was plenty experienced, too.

When the one dance was over, another tune started right away and he swung her into a country waltz. She found herself laughing as they danced and then she realized her headache had vanished. Every touch of his hands sent warmth throughout her body. Or was that just the heat of her skin from dancing?

She was ready to walk off the dance floor the moment the next song struck up, a slow tune, but Creed took her by the hand then brought her into his arms, catching her off guard. She braced her palms on his shoulders to keep him from holding her too close. He leaned down to whisper in her ear.

His warm breath caused a shiver to run through her as he murmured, "Thank you for the dances."

She swallowed, trying to not let his closeness affect her…the solidness of his body, his masculine scent, and the heat of his large hands at her waist. She cleared her throat but couldn't get anything out.

"I'd like to see you again," he said close to her ear.

She drew back and gave him a skeptical look. "You're a bull rider. You don't stay in one place for too long."

"Long enough," he said. "Where are you from?"

"I'm from southern Arizona, in the San Rafael Valley," she said. "But I now live in San Diego."

"There you go." He gave her a little grin. "We do have something in common. I'm from just north of Phoenix, in Kirkland, between Prescott and Wickenburg." He touched a lock of her long, dark hair. "What's an Arizona country girl doing in San Diego?"

"I work as a research associate at the University of California," she said. "In our department we do breeding maintenance, genotyping, cloning, and other related projects."

"I'm impressed." He continued to lightly play with her hair. "Did you go to the University of Arizona?"

She nodded. "Yes."

"I graduated from the U of A twelve years ago," he said with a grin. "I'd bet you were at least eight years behind me."

"Something like that." She smiled. "What was your major?"

"Animal Sciences."

The song ended, surprising her. The time had passed faster than she'd expected.

"I'd better go," she said as they drew apart.

"Why?" He walked beside her as she left the dance floor.

"It's getting late." And she was becoming far too interested in this bull rider.

He caught her by her hand and drew her to a stop. "Sure I can't talk you into a drink?"

"You already talked me into dancing with you." She smiled. "But no, not a drink."

"Give me your phone number," he said. "I want to see you again."

She shook her head. "I don't date bull riders."

With a laugh he said, "Why not?"

"It's too dangerous a sport," she said. "I'd be worried all the time."

"You'd worry about me?" He had that sexy grin again.

Somehow she felt off-balance by his reply. "I suppose I would, if we were dating. Which isn't a possibility because, like I said, I don't date bull riders."

"Why don't you give me a chance?" he said. "I'll show you that you don't have to worry about me."

She put her hands on her hips. "How many bones have you broken over the years? How many concussions have you had? How many times have you had to be stitched up?"

He winced.

"Or," she went on, "maybe you should just tell me what bones you *haven't* broken. Yet."

He shook his head. "It's not as bad as it sounds."

"Oh?" She folded her arms across her chest. "How many times have you ridden even when you were injured rather than waiting for those bones and injuries to heal?" She didn't wait for an answer. "More times than you can count, I'll bet."

He laughed and raised his hands. "Aw, come on, Danica. Just give me a chance."

She liked the way he said her name. His voice had a raw, sensual quality about it. "I'm heading up to my room now," she said. "It really was nice meeting you."

"So you're staying here," he said as she turned away and he fell into step beside her.

She realized her mistake when she'd said "up to my room." She paused mid-step and shook her head as she faced him. "Good night, Creed."

"I know when I'm not wanted." A smile was on his lips though when he said the words. "Good night, Danica."

As she walked out of the bar and made her way to the elevators, she found it hard not to look over her shoulder. She could feel him watching her and if she looked, she might find herself turning around and going back.

About Cheyenne

New York Times and *USA Today* bestselling author Cheyenne McCray's books have received multiple awards and nominations, including

*RT *Book Reviews* magazine's Reviewer's Choice awards for Best Erotic Romance of the year and Best Paranormal Action Adventure of the year

*Three "RT Book Reviews" nominations, including Best Erotic Romance, Best Romantic Suspense, and Best Paranormal Action Adventure.

*Golden Quill award for Best Erotic Romance

*The Road to Romance's Reviewer's Choice Award

*Gold Star Award from Just Erotic Romance Reviews

*CAPA award from The Romance Studio

Cheyenne grew up on a ranch in southeastern Arizona. She has been writing ever since she can remember, back to her kindergarten days when she penned her first poem. She always knew one day she would write novels, hoping her readers would get lost in the worlds she created, just as she experienced when she read some of her favorite books.

Chey has three sons, two dogs, and is an Arizona native who loves the desert, the sunshine, and the beautiful sunsets. Visit Chey's website and get all of the latest info at her website and meet up with her at Cheyenne McCray's Place on Facebook!

CPSIA information can be obtained at www.ICGtesting.com
Printed in the USA
LVOW051530190213

320796LV00001B/154/P